B53

D1100467

Revelations

BY MELISSA DE LA CRUZ

Blue Bloods
Masquerade
Revelations
The Van Alen Legacy

Keys to the Repository

Revelations

A
Blue Bloods
NOVEL

Melissa de la Cruz

www.atombooks.co.uk

ATOM

First published in the United States in 2009 by Hyperion
First published in Great Britain in 2010 by Atom
Reprinted 2010 (four times)

Copyright © 2008 by Melissa de la Cruz

Extract from *The Van Alen Legacy* by Melissa de la Cruz
Copyright © 2008 by Melissa de la Cruz

The moral right of the author has been asserted.

*All characters and events in this publication, other than those
clearly in the public domain, are fictitious and any resemblance
to real persons, living or dead, is purely coincidental.*

All rights reserved.
No part of this publication may be reproduced, stored in a
retrieval system, or transmitted, in any form or by any means, without
the prior permission in writing of the publisher, nor be otherwise circulated
in any form of binding or cover other than that in which it is published
and without a similar condition including this condition being
imposed on the subsequent purchaser.

A CIP catalogue record for this book
is available from the British Library.

ISBN 978-1-905654-78-9

Printed and bound in Great Britain by
Clays Ltd, St Ives plc

Papers used by Atom are natural, renewable and
recyclable products sourced from well-managed forests and certified
in accordance with the rules of the Forest Stewardship Council.

Mixed Sources
Product group from well-managed
forests and other controlled sources
www.fsc.org   Cert no. SGS-COC-004081
© 1996 Forest Stewardship Council
FSC

Atom
An imprint of
Little, Brown Book Group
100 Victoria Embankment
London EC4Y 0DY

An Hachette UK Company
www.hachette.co.uk

www.atombooks.net

For Mike & Mattie, always

And for Stephen Green and Carol Fox, my "oldest" fans

ROTHERHAM LIBRARY SERVICE	
B53010844	
Bertrams	19/02/2012
JF	£6.99
BSU	

The Van Alen Family Tree

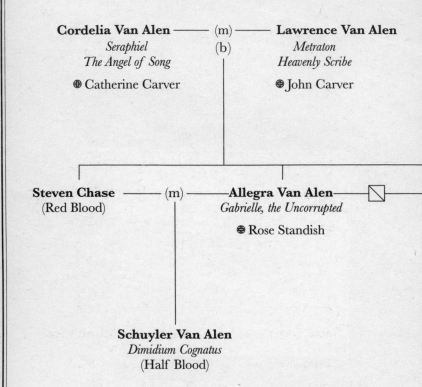

Cordelia Van Alen —— (m) —— **Lawrence Van Alen**
Seraphiel   (b)   *Metraton*
The Angel of Song   *Heavenly Scribe*

⊕ Catherine Carver   ⊕ John Carver

Steven Chase —— (m) —— **Allegra Van Alen**
(Red Blood)   *Gabrielle, the Uncorrupted*

                             ⊕ Rose Standish

Schuyler Van Alen
Dimidium Cognatus
(Half Blood)

$\square$ = Broken bond

(m) = Married

(b) = Immortal bond

$\oplus$ = Known name from past lives

Charles (Van Alen) Force ——(m)—— **Trinity Burden Force**
Michael, Pure of Heart

$\oplus$ Myles Standish

Benjamin (Jack) Force ——(b)—— **Madeleine (Mimi) Force**
Abbadon   *Azrael*
The Angel of Destruction   *The Angel of Death*

$\oplus$ Valerius $\oplus$ Agrippina
$\oplus$ Louis D'Orleans $\oplus$ Elisabeth Lorraine-Lillebonne
$\oplus$ William White $\oplus$ Susannah Fuller

The greatest test of courage is to bear defeat without losing heart.

—Robert G. Ingersoll

O you were a vampire and I may never see the light.

—Concrete Blonde, "Bloodletting"

Now war arose in heaven,
Michael and his angels fighting against the dragon;
and the dragon and his angels fought,
but they were defeated and there was no longer
any place for them in heaven. . . .
"But woe to you, O earth and sea,
for the devil has come down to you in great wrath,
because he knows that his time is short!"

—Revelation 12:7–12

THE BATTLE OF CORCOVADO

She looked up and saw Lawrence locked in a fierce struggle with his adversary. His sword fell to the ground. Above him loomed the white, shining presence. It was so bright it was blinding, like looking into the sun. It was the Lightbringer. The Morningstar.

Her blood froze.

"Schuyler!" Oliver's voice was hoarse. "Kill it!"

Schuyler raised her mother's sword, saw it glinting in the moonlight, a long, pale, deadly shaft. Raised it in the direction of the enemy. Ran with all her might and thrust her weapon toward his heart.

And missed.

<<hissing sound, then an audible *click*>>

I have secured position in Target Area and will commence investigation into death by consumption of Augusta Carondolet. Victim was found fully drained at New York nightclub, The Bank. The following persons of interest were in the area on the night of attack:

Schuyler Van Alen: Half-Blood, mortal father of no distinction; Mother: Allegra Van Alen (Gabrielle); Fifteen years of age.

Bliss Llewellyn: Cycle daughter of Senator Forsyth Llewellyn; Birth records indicate mother unnamed (Is this correct?); Fifteen years of age.

Madeleine Force: Cycle daughter of Charles Force (Michael) and Trinity Burden Force; Sixteen years of age. Twin brother Benjamin Force also in vicinity the night of 9/12, yet has been removed from suspect list as confirmed he had vacated the premises before the attack.

EXTREMELY DELICATE situation as this suspect is daughter of current Regis. Do not disclose suspect list to Regis until fully confirmed.

Initial suspect, Dylan Ward, still at large; whereabouts: unknown.

ONE

On an early and bitterly cold morning in late March, Schuyler Van Alen let herself inside the glass doors of the Duchesne School, feeling relieved as she walked into the soaring barrel-ceiling entryway dominated by an imposing John Singer Sargent portrait of the school's founders. She kept the hood of her fur-trimmed parka over her thick dark hair, preferring anonymity rather than the casual greetings exchanged by other students.

It was odd to think of the school as a haven, an escape, a place she looked forward to going. For so long, Duchesne, with its shiny marble floors and sweeping vistas of Central Park, was nothing less than a torture chamber. She had dreaded walking up the grand staircase, felt miserable in its inadequately heated classrooms, and even managed to despise the gorgeous terrazzo tiles in the refectory.

At school Schuyler often felt ugly and invisible, although

her deep-set blue eyes and delicate Dresden-doll features belied this. All her life, her well-heeled classmates had treated her like a freak, an outcast—unwanted and untouchable. Even if her family was one of the oldest and most illustrious names in the city's history, times had changed. The Van Alens, once a proud and prestigious clan, had shrunk and withered over the centuries, so that they were now practically extinct. Schuyler was one of the last.

For a while, Schuyler had hoped her grandfather's return from exile would change that—that Lawrence's presence in her life would mean she was no longer alone. But those hopes were dashed when Charles Force took her away from the shabby brownstone on Riverside Drive, the only home she had ever known.

"Are you going to move or do I have to do something about it?"

Schuyler started. She hadn't noticed that she'd been standing in a daze in front of her locker and the one above it. The bells signaling the start of the day were clanging wildly. Behind her stood Mimi Force, her new housemate.

No matter how out of place Schuyler felt at school, it was no comparison to the arctic freeze she weathered on a daily basis at the Forces' grand town house across from the Metropolitan Museum. At Duchesne, she didn't have to overhear Mimi grumbling about her every second of the day. Or at least it only happened every few hours. No wonder Duchesne felt so welcoming lately.

Even though Lawrence Van Alen was now Regis, head of the Blue Bloods, he had been powerless to stop the adoption process. The Code of the Vampires stipulated a strict adherence to human laws, to keep the Blue Bloods safe from unwanted scrutiny. In her last will and testament, Schuyler's grandmother had declared her an emancipated minor, but in a wily move, Charles Force's lawyers had contested its tenets in the Red Blood courts. The courts found in their favor, and Charles had been named the executor of the estate, winning Schuyler as part of the package.

"Well?" Mimi was still waiting.

"Oh. Uh. Sorry," Schuyler said, grabbing a textbook and moving aside.

"Sorry is right," Mimi narrowed her emerald green eyes and gave Schuyler a contemptuous look. The same look she'd given Schuyler across the dinner table last night, and the same look she'd given Schuyler when they'd bumped into each other in the hallway that morning. The look said: *What are you doing here? You have no right to exist.*

"What did I ever do to you?" Schuyler whispered, tucking a book into her worn canvas bag.

"You saved her life!"

Mimi glared at the striking redhead who had spoken.

Bliss Llewellyn, Texan transplant and former Mimi acolyte, glared back. Bliss's cheeks were as red as her hair. "She saved your skin in Venice, and you don't even have the decency to be grateful!" Once upon a time Bliss had been

Mimi's shadow, happy to follow her every directive, but a trust had broken between the two former friends since the last Silver Blood attack, when Mimi had been revealed as a willing, if ineffective, conspirator. Mimi had been condemned to burn, until Schuyler had come to her aid at the blood trial.

"She didn't save my life. She merely told the truth. My life was never in danger," Mimi replied as she ran a silver hairbrush through her fine hair.

"Ignore her," Bliss told Schuyler.

Schuyler smiled, feeling braver now that she had backup. "It's hard to do. It's like pretending global warming doesn't exist." She would pay for that comment later, she knew. There would be pebbles in her breakfast cereal. Black tar on her sheets. Or the newest inconvenience—the disappearance of yet another of her swiftly dwindling possessions. Already she was missing her mother's locket, her leather gloves, and a beloved dog-eared copy of Kafka's *The Trial*, inscribed on the first page with the initials "J. F."

Schuyler would be the first to admit that the second guest bedroom in the Forces' mansion (the first remained reserved for visiting dignitaries) was hardly the cupboard under the stairs. Her room was beautifully decorated and sumptuously appointed with everything a girl could want: a four-poster queen-size bed with a pillowy duvet, closets full of designer clothes, a high-end entertainment center, dozens of toys for Beauty, her bloodhound, and a new featherlight

MacBook Air. But if her new home was rich in material gifts, it lacked the charm of the old one.

She missed her old room, with its Mountain Dew–yellow walls and rickety desk. She missed the dusty shrouded living room. She missed Hattie and Julius, who had been with the family since she was an infant. She missed her grandfather, of course. But most of all, she missed her freedom.

"You okay?" Bliss asked, nudging her. Schuyler had returned from Venice with a new address and an unexpected ally. While she and Bliss had always been friendly, now they were almost inseparable.

"Yeah. I'm used to it. I could take her in a cage fight." Schuyler smiled. Seeing Bliss at school was one of the small reprieves of happiness that Duchesne afforded.

She took the winding back stairs, following the stream of people heading in the same direction, when out of the corner of her eye she saw the barest flicker and knew. It was him. She didn't have to look to know he was among the crowd of students walking the opposite way. She could always sense him, as if her nerves were fine-tuned antennae receptors that picked up whenever he was near. Maybe it was the vampire in her, giving her the ability to tell when another was close by, or maybe it had nothing to do with her otherworldly powers at all.

Jack.

His eyes were focused straight ahead, as if he never even saw her, never registered her presence. His sleek blond hair, the same translucent shade as his sister's, was slicked back from his proud forehead; and unlike the other boys around him, dressed in varying degrees of sloppiness, he looked regal in a blazer and tie. He was so handsome it was hard for Schuyler to breathe. But just as at the town house—Schuyler refused to call it *home*—Jack ignored her.

She snuck one more glance his way and then hurried up the stairs. Class had already started when she arrived. Schuyler tried to be as unobtrusive as possible as she walked, out of habit, toward the back seats by the window. Oliver Hazard-Perry was seated there, bent over his notebook.

But she caught herself just in time and moved across the room to sit next to the clanging radiator, without saying hello to her best friend.

Charles Force had made it clear: now that she was under his roof, she would have to follow his rules. The first rule was that Schuyler was forbidden to see her grandfather. The animosity between Charles and Lawrence ran deep, and not only because Lawrence had displaced Charles's position in the Conclave.

"I don't want him filling your head with lies," Charles had told her. "He may rule the Coven, but he has no power in my house. If you disobey me, I promise you will regret it."

The second rule of living at the Forces' was that she was forbidden to associate with Oliver. Charles had been apoplectic when he'd discovered that Schuyler had made Oliver (her designated Conduit) her human familiar. "First

8

of all, you are much too young. Secondly, it is *anathema*. Distasteful. Conduits are servants. They are not—they do not fulfill the services of familiars. You must take a new human immediately and sever all relations with this boy."

If pressed, she would grudgingly admit that Charles was probably right. Oliver was her best friend, and she had marked him as her own, had taken his blood into hers, and there had been consequences to her actions. Sometimes she wished they could go back to the way they were before everything became so complicated.

Schuyler had no idea why Charles would care whom she made her familiar anyway, since the Forces had done away with the old-fashioned practice of keeping human Conduits. But she followed the rules to the letter. As far as anyone could see, she had absolutely no contact with Lawrence, and had refrained from performing the Sacred Kiss with Oliver.

There were so many things in her new life that she could and couldn't do.

But there were some places where the rules did not apply. Somewhere that Charles had no power. Somewhere Schuyler could be free.

That's what secret hiding places were for.

TWO

*M*imi Force liked the sound of stilettos on marble. Her patent-leather Jimmy Choos made a satisfying click, click, clack that echoed across the entire lobby of the Force Tower. The shiny new headquarters of her father's media empire comprised several buildings in the middle of midtown Manhattan. The gleaming elevator banks regularly disgorged a crew of "Forcies"—the beautiful employees of the Force media organization—design editors, fashion editors, lifestyle editors, heading off to lunch meetings at Michael's or into town cars that would escort them to various appointments around the city. They were a well-dressed group, with similarly pinched faces, as if their perpetually busy schedules didn't leave them time to smile. Mimi blended right in.

She was only sixteen, but as she walked through the crowd, past the lobby and into the dark alcove that concealed an elevator that could only be accessed through a secret and irreproducible key, she felt incredibly *old*. She remembered when the Force Tower had originally been christened the Van Alen Building. For years it had stood as a mere three-story foundation, since its planned tower had never been built after the Crash of 1929 and the Great Depression. Only last year did her father's company finally complete construction according to the old plans and christened the building with a new name.

Mimi looked around and discreetly sent a strong ignore-suggestion to anyone who might come near. She found the doorknob and pressed her finger against the lock, pricking it so that it drew blood. The blood analysis in the key lock was not the latest in security technology, but an antediluvian one. Her blood was being analyzed and compared to DNA files in the repository; a match would confirm that only a true Blue Blood stood at the gate. The blood could not be duplicated nor extracted. Vampire blood disappeared within minutes once exposed to the air.

The doors whooshed open silently, and Mimi took the lift down. What Red Bloods did not know was that in 1929, the building *had* been built to completion—except it extended downward instead of up.

The tower was actually a "corescraper"—a structure built underneath the ground, tunneling down to the planet's core, rather than up toward the sky. Mimi watched as the floors descended. She went fifty, then a hundred, then two hundred, then a thousand feet under the surface. In the past, the Blue Bloods had lived underground to hide from their Silver Blood attackers. Now Mimi understood what Charles Force had meant when he sneered that Lawrence and Cordelia would have the vampires "cringing in caves once again."

Finally the elevator stopped and the door opened. Mimi nodded to the Conduit at the desk. The Red Blood resembled a blind mole rat, looking as if he had not seen the sun in a long time. Rather like the false legends perpetuated about vampires, Mimi thought with amusement.

She could feel the wards, the heavy protections placed around the area. This was supposed to be the Blue Bloods' most secret and secure haven. Lawrence took great pleasure in the shiny, conspicuous new tower that had been built on top of it. "We're hiding in plain sight!" he'd chuckled. The Repository of History had recently been moved to several of the lower floors. Since the attack, the lair underneath the club had been abandoned. Mimi still felt guilty at what had happened there. But it wasn't her fault! She hadn't meant to bring any real harm. She'd just wanted Schuyler out of the way. Perhaps she had been naive. No need to linger on that thought now.

"Evening, Madeleine," an elegantly dressed woman in a chic Chanel suit greeted her politely.

"Dorothea." Mimi nodded, following the old crone to the conference room. She knew that several members of the

Conclave had not been keen on her admittance to the inner circle. They were worried she was still too young and not in command of her full memories, the entirety of the wisdom of all her past lives. The process toward a Blue Blood's complete self-actualization began during the transformation at fifteen, and continued until the end of one's Sunset Years (or approximately twenty-one years of age), when the human shell fully gave away, finally revealing the vampire underneath. Mimi didn't care what they thought. She was there to fulfill a duty, and if she didn't remember everything, she remembered *enough*.

She was there because Lawrence had come to the Force mansion late one night, soon after they'd returned from Venice, to speak to Charles. Mimi had overhead the entire conversation. When Lawrence had taken over as Regis, Charles had voluntarily resigned his seat on the Conclave, but Lawrence was urging him to reconsider.

"We need all our strength now. We need you, Charles. Don't turn your back on us." Lawrence's voice was low and gravelly. He coughed several times, and the smell of sweet tobacco from his pipe had filled the hallway outside her father's office.

Charles was adamant. He had been humiliated and rejected. If the Conclave would not have him, he would not have the Conclave. "Why do they need me when they have you, *Regis*," Charles spat, as if even saying it were distasteful.

"I will go."

Lawrence had merely raised an eyebrow upon discovering Mimi standing in front of them. Charles hadn't looked too surprised either. Finding a way through locked doors had always been one of Mimi's talents, even as a young child.

"Azrael," Lawrence murmured. "Do you remember?"

"Not everything. Not yet. But I do remember you . . . *Grandfather*," Mimi said with a smirk.

"That's enough for me." Lawrence smiled in a way that was not too unlike Charles's own. "Charles, it's decided. Mimi shall have your seat on the Conclave. She will report to you, as your representative. Azrael, you are dismissed."

Mimi had been about to protest, until she realized she had been glommed into leaving the den without her noticing. The old coot was clever. But nothing was stopping her from pressing an ear against the doors.

"She is dangerous," Lawrence was saying softly. "I was surprised to find that you had called up the twins to this cycle. Was it really necessary?"

"Like you said, she is strong." Charles sighed. "If there *is* battle ahead, as you want us all to believe, Lawrence, you will need her on your side."

Lawrence snorted. "If she stays true."

"She always has," Charles said sharply. "And she was not the only one among us who once loved the Morningstar."

"A grave mistake we all made." Lawrence nodded.

Charles said softly, "No, not all of us."

14

Mimi floated away from the door. She had heard all she needed to hear.

Azrael. He'd called her by her real name. A name that was etched deep into her consciousness, deep into her bones, her very blood. What was she except her name? When you were alive for thousands of years, taking a new moniker after another, names became like gift wrapping. Something decorative that you answered to. Take her name in this cycle, for example: Mimi. It was the name of a socialite, a flighty woman who spent her days maxing out credit cards and who cared only for spa treatments and dinner parties.

It hid her true identity.

For she was Azrael. Angel of Death. She brought darkness to the light. It was her gift and her curse.

She was a Blue Blood. As Charles had said, one of the strongest. Charles and Lawrence had been talking about the end of days. The Fall. During the war with Lucifer, it had been Azrael and her twin, Abbadon, who had turned the tide, who had changed the course of the last battle. They had betrayed their prince and joined Michael, kneeling to the golden sword. They had stayed true to the light, even though they were made of the dark.

Theirs had been a crucial desertion. If it were not for her and Jack, who could say who would have won? Would Lucifer be the king of all kings on a heavenly throne if they had not abandoned him? And what did they win anyway, but this endless life on earth. This endless cycle of reparation and absolution. For whom and for what did they make amends? Did God even know they existed anymore? Would they ever regain the paradise they had lost?

Had it been worth it? Mimi wondered as she took her seat at the Conclave, only now noticing the grumblings among her peers.

She looked to where Dorothea Rockefeller was staring. The shock almost sent her reeling. Inside the most protected, most secure haven of the Blue Bloods, and seated next to Lawrence in a place of honor, was none other than the disgraced former Venator, the Silver Blood traitor, Kingsley Martin.

He caught her eye and pointed two fingers in the shape of a gun in her direction. And Kingsley being Kingsley, he smiled as he pretended to pull the trigger.

$\mathcal{U}$nlike most designers' showrooms, which were decorated in minimal, almost clinical style with hardly a floral arrangement to break up the dazzlingly empty white rooms, the showcase interiors that housed the Rolf Morgan collection resembled the cozy quarters of an old-fashioned gentlemen's club: leather-bound books lined the shelves, while squat club chairs and comfortable shag rugs were arranged around a crackling fire. Rolf Morgan had come to fame by selling preppie, old-boy style to the masses, his most ubiquitous creation a plain-collared shirt discreetly embroidered with his logo: a pair of criss-crossed croquet wickets.

Bliss sat nervously on one of the leather armchairs, balancing her portfolio on her knees. She'd had to leave school a few minutes early in order to make her go-see appointment, yet had arrived to find the designer running half an hour late. Typical.

She looked around at the other models, all bearing the same classic American good looks commonly found in a "Croquet by Rolf Morgan" ad: sunburned cheeks, golden hair, upturned button noses. She had no idea why the designer would be interested in her. Bliss looked more like a girl from a pre-Raphaelite painting, with her waist-long russet hair, pale skin, and wide green eyes, than the kind of girl who looked like she'd just finished a rousing set of tennis. But then again, Schuyler had just booked the show the other day at the first casting, so perhaps they were looking for a different kind of girl this time.

"Can I get you girls anything? Water? Diet soda?" the smiling receptionist asked.

"Nothing for me, thanks," Bliss demurred, while the other girls shook their heads as well. It was nice to be asked, to be offered something. As a model, she was used to being ignored or condescended to by the staff. No one was ever very friendly. Bliss likened go-see appointments to the cattle inspections her grandfather used to perform on the ranch. He'd check the stock's teeth, hooves, and flanks. Models were treated just like cattle—pieces of meat whose assets were weighed and measured.

Bliss wished that the designer would hurry up and get it over with. She'd almost canceled the meeting, and only a deep sense of obligation to her agency (and a slight fear of her model booker—a bald, imperious gay man, who bossed her around like she was his slave (and not the other way around) kept her rooted to her seat.

She was still unnerved by what had happened at school earlier, when she'd tried to confide in Schuyler.

"There's something wrong with me," Bliss said, over lunch in the refectory.

"What do you mean? Are you sick?" Schuyler asked, ripping open a bag of jalapeño potato chips.

Am I sick? Bliss wondered. She certainly felt ill lately. But it was a different kind of sick—her *soul* felt sick. "It's hard to explain," she said, but she tried. "I'm, like, seeing things. Bad things." Terrible things. She told Schuyler about how it had started.

She'd been jogging down the Hudson the other day, and when she blinked, instead of the placid, brown waters of the river, she'd seen it filled with blood—red and viscous and churning.

Then there were the horsemen who had thundered into her bedroom one night—four of them, on tall black steeds, behind masks; they looked foul and smelled even worse. Like living death. They had been so real, the horses had left dirty hoofprints on the white carpet. But the vision from the other night had been worse: bayoneted babies, disemboweled victims, nuns hanging from crosses, beheaded . . . It went on.

But the most frightening thing in the world?

Right in the middle of a vision, a man had appeared. A man in a white suit. A handsome man, with a crown of shining golden hair and a beautiful smile that chilled her to the bone.

The man had walked across the room and sat next to her on the bed.

"Bliss," the man had said, laying a hand on her head like a benediction. "Daughter."

Schuyler looked up from her tuna sandwich. Bliss wondered how Schuyler still had an appetite for normal food—Bliss had long ago lost the taste for it. She could barely stand to eat her rare-cooked hamburger. Maybe it was because Schuyler was half human. Bliss reached for a potato chip out of curiosity. She took a bite. It was salty and not unpleasantly spicy. She took another.

Schuyler looked thoughtful. "Okay, so some weird dude called you his daughter, big deal. It was just a dream. And as for all the other stuff—are you sure you're not just staying up too late watching Rob Zombie movies?"

"No—it just . . ." Bliss shook her head, annoyed at being unable to impart just how creepy this man was. And how it sounded like he was telling her the truth. But how could that be? Her father was Forsyth Llewellyn, the senator from New York. She wondered about her mother once again. Her father never spoke of his first wife, and just a few weeks ago Bliss had been surprised to find a photograph of her father with a blond woman who she'd always assumed to be her mother inscribed on the back with the words "Allegra Van Alen."

Allegra was Schuyler's mother, New York City's most famous comatose patient. If Allegra was her mother, did that make Schuyler her sister? Although, vampires didn't have family in the Red Blood sense: they were the former children of God, immortal, with no real mothers and fathers.

Forsyth was merely her "father" for this cycle. Perhaps that was the same with Allegra. She'd refrained from telling Schuyler her discovery. Schuyler was protective about her mother, and Bliss was too shy to claim a connection to a woman she had never even met. Still, she'd felt a kinship to Schuyler ever since she'd found the photograph.

"Do you still get those—you know, blackouts?" Schuyler asked.

Bliss shook her head. The blackouts had stopped at about the same time the visions had begun. She didn't know what was worse.

"Sky, do you ever think about Dylan?" she asked tentatively.

"All the time. I wish I knew what happened to him," Schuyler said, picking apart her sandwich and eating it one section at a time: bread first, then a scoop of tuna, then a bite of the lettuce. "I miss him. He was a good friend."

Bliss nodded. She wondered how she could broach the subject. She had been keeping a huge secret for too long now. Dylan, whom everyone had given up for dead, who'd been taken by a Silver Blood, who'd completely disappeared . . . had come back, crashing through her window just two weeks ago and telling her the most outrageous stories. Ever since the night he had returned, Bliss didn't know what to believe.

Dylan had to be completely mental. Crazy. What he'd said that night. It just didn't make sense, but he was convinced it was the god's honest truth. She could never talk him out of it, and lately he'd been threatening to do something. Just that morning he'd been seriously unhinged. Raving. Shouting like a maniac. It had been hard to watch. She'd promised him she would . . . she would . . . what would she do? She had no idea.

"Bliss Llewellyn?"

"Here," Bliss replied, standing and tucking her portfolio under her arm.

"We're ready for you. Sorry for the wait."

"Not a problem," she said, giving them her most professional smile. She followed the girl into an airy room in the back. Bliss had to walk what seemed like the length of a football field to reach the small table where the designer was seated.

It was always like this. They liked to watch you walk, and after you said hello, they'd ask you to just turn around and walk again. Rolf was casting for his Fashion Week show, and seated next to him were his team: a tanned, blond woman wearing dark glasses, a thin effeminate man, and several assistants.

"Hi, Bliss," Rolf said. "This is my wife, Randy, and this is Cyrus, who's putting the show together."

"Hi." Bliss offered her hand and shook his firmly.

"We're well acquainted with your work," Rolf said, taking a cursory glance at her photographs. He was a deeply tanned man with salt-and-pepper hair. When he crossed his arms, his muscles bulged. He looked like a cowboy, down to his custom-made alligator boots. That is, if cowboys got their tans in St. Barth's and their shirts made in Hong Kong. "In fact, we're pretty sure you're the girl for us. We just wanted to meet you."

Instead of putting Bliss at ease, the designer's friendliness made her even more nervous. The job was now hers to lose. "Oh, um, okay."

Randy Morgan, the designer's wife, was the quintessential "Morgan girl," down to the windswept hair. Bliss knew she had been Rolf's first model, back in the seventies, and still occasionally starred in some of the advertising campaigns. Randy pushed her sunglasses on top of her head and gave Bliss a brilliant smile. "The brand is going in a different direction for the show. We want to set an Edwardian mood— old-fashioned romance. There's going to be a lot of velvet, a lot of lace, maybe even a corset or two in the collection. We wanted a girl who didn't look too contemporary."

Bliss nodded, not quite sure what they were getting at,

since every other brand that had booked her in the past thought she had looked "contemporary" enough. "Do you want me to walk or . . . ?"

"Please."

Bliss headed to the back of the room, took a deep breath, and began to walk. She walked as if she were walking in the moors at night, as if she were alone in the fog. As if she were a bit lost and dreamy. And just as she hit the pivot marker, the room spun and she had another vision.

Like she'd told Schuyler, she never had blackouts anymore. She could still see the showroom, as well as the designer and his team. Yet there it was: seated in the middle between Rolf and his wife was a crimson-eyed beast with a silver forked tongue. Maggots were crawling out of its eyes. She wanted to scream. Instead she closed her eyes and kept walking.

When she opened her eyes, Rolf and his team were clapping.

Apocalyptic visions or not, Bliss was hired.

Four

"I missed you." Oliver's lips against her cheek were warm and soft, and Schuyler felt a sharp ache in her stomach at the depth of his affection.

"I missed you too," she whispered back. That was true enough. They had not been together like this for a fortnight. And while she wanted to press her lips against his neck and do what came naturally, she stopped herself. She didn't need it right now, and she was wary of doing it because of how it made her feel. The *Caerimonia Osculor* was a drug—tempting and irresistible. It gave her too much power. Too much power over him.

She couldn't. Not here. Not now. Later. Maybe. Besides, it wasn't safe. They were in the supply closet off the copy room. Anyone could walk in and catch the two of them together. They had met, like they always did, in between the first and second bell after fourth period. They had all of five minutes.

"Will you be there . . . tonight?" Oliver asked, his voice husky in her ear. She wanted to run her fingers through his thick, caramel-colored hair, but she restrained herself. Instead she pressed her nose against the side of his head. He smelled so clean.

How had they been friends for so long without her knowing what his hair smelled like? But now she knew: like grass after the rain. He smelled so good she could cry. She had failed him in every way. He would never forgive her if he truly understood what she had done to him.

"I don't know," Schuyler replied, hesitating. "I'll try." She wanted to let him down as gently as she could. She looked into his genial, handsome face, his warm hazel eyes flecked with brown and gold.

"Promise," Oliver's voice was cold. "Promise." He pressed her tightly against him, and she was surprised at his strength. She had no idea humans could be just as strong as vampires when the occasion arose.

Her heart tore. Charles Force was right. She should keep away from him. Someone was going to get hurt, and she couldn't bear to think of Oliver suffering because of her. She wasn't worth it. "Ollie, you know I—"

"Don't say it. Just be there," he said roughly, and let go of her so quickly she almost lost her balance. Then he was gone just as fast, leaving her alone in the dark room, feeling strangely bereft.

* * *

Later that evening Schuyler zipped through the dark rainy streets, a blur of silver in her new raincoat. She could take a cab, but there were none to be had in the rain, and she preferred to walk—or rather, glide. She liked to flex her vampire muscles, liked how fast she could be when she set her mind to it. She'd walked the entire length of the island like a cat; she'd moved so quickly she had stayed dry. There was not a drop of wet on her.

The building was one of those new dazzling glass apartment buildings designed by the architect Richard Meier on the corner of Perry Street and the West Side Highway. They gleamed like crystal in the dark foggy twilight. Schuyler never got tired of looking at them, they were so beautiful.

Schuyler slipped inside the side doors, relishing the vampire speed that rendered her invisible to the guard and the other residents. She passed on the elevator, preferring to use her otherworldly talents and run up the back stairs, taking the steps four, five, sometimes ten at a time. In seconds she was in the penthouse.

It was warm in the apartment, and the streetlights below illuminated everything inside the floor-to-ceiling glass windows. She pressed the button to automatically draw the curtains. They'd left them open again, exposed—amazing how their secret hiding place was located in one of the most visible buildings in Manhattan.

The housekeeper had set out logs for the fireplace, so

Schuyler made a quick fire, easy as pushing another button. The flames rose high and licked at the wood. Schuyler watched it burn; then, as if seeing her future in the flames, put her head in her hands.

What was she doing here?

Why had she come?

It was wrong, what they were doing. He knew it. She knew it. They had told each other it would be for the last time. As if they would be able to bear it. She was both ecstatic and sorrowful at the prospect of their meeting.

Schuyler busied herself by emptying the dishwasher and setting the table. Lighting the candles. She hooked up the stereo to her iPod, and soon Rufus Wainwright's voice echoed through the walls. It was a song of yearning—their favorite.

She contemplated a bath, knowing her robe was hanging on a hook in the closet. There was so little evidence of their presence in the place—a few books, a set of clothes, a couple of toothbrushes. This was not a home, this was a secret.

She looked at herself in the mirror—her hair was mussed and her eyes were bright. He would be here soon. Of course he would. He was the one who had insisted.

The designated hour passed, yet no one arrived. Schuyler tucked her knees against her chest, trying to fight the rising tide of disappointment.

She had almost dropped off to sleep when there was a shadow on the terrace.

Schuyler looked up expectantly, feeling a mixture of anticipation and a deep and abiding sadness. Her heart was racing a million miles a minute. Even if she saw him every day, it would always be like the first time.

"Hey, you," a voice said. And a boy appeared from the shadows.

But he was not the one she was waiting for.

Schuyler Van Alen: Noticeable alienation from peers. Prefers the company of her Conduit, human male: Oliver Hazard-Perry. Survivor of two possible Silver Blood attacks. Will continue to monitor, yet am convinced it is unlikely she is the guilty party.

Bliss Llewellyn: Interesting case. Complains of headaches, dizziness, "blackouts." Perhaps side effect of transformation? Was discovered drowning in Central Park lake night of 11/28. Managed to rescue subject without revealing cover.

Madeleine Force: Possesses significant dark power and displays flagrant disregard for rules, especially those concerning human familiars.

UPDATE ON DYLAN WARD:
Long Island team reports subject sighted fleeing the Ward house on Shelter Island. Have sent reinforcements to bring him in.

*T*he meeting was convened in regular fashion. The secretary took roll. All the old families were repre-sented, the original seven (Van Alen, Cutler, Oelrich, Van Horn, Schlumberger, Stewart, and Rockefeller) had grown to accommodate the Llewellyns, the Duponts (represented by a nervous-looking Eliza, who was the late Priscilla's niece), the Whitneys, and the Carondolets. This was the Conclave of Elders—the gathering of the Blue Blood elite. This was where the decisions for the race, for the future of the clan, were made.

Lawrence welcomed them to the first spring session with a hearty greeting, and began to run through the agenda items: the upcoming fund-raiser for the New York Blood Bank, the latest news on blood-borne diseases and how they would affect the Blue Bloods, how their trust accounts were doing—Blue Blood money was invested heavily in the stock market, and the latest downturn had caused several millions of dollars to disappear.

Mimi was beside herself. Lawrence conducted the meeting as if nothing were amiss, as if a traitor weren't sitting next to him. It was maddening! It had been Kingsley who had called the Silver Blood, Kingsley who had arranged the attack at the Repository, Kingsley who had been the mastermind behind the cover-up, and yet there he was, seated at the table as if he belonged.

On the surface, the Conclave was as calm and placid and nonplussed as ever, although Mimi could detect a slight unease, just the faintest whiff of discord within the ranks. Why didn't Lawrence say anything? The old coot was babbling about the sub-prime market and the recent disastrous events on Wall Street. Ah, finally . . . Lawrence turned to Kingsley. An explanation at last.

But no. Lawrence matter-of-factly declared that Kingsley had a report to file, and ceded the floor to the so-called *Venator*, a Truth-Teller, a member of the vampire secret police.

Kingsley acknowledged the table with a grim smile. "Elders . . . and um, Mimi," he began. He was just as wickedly handsome as ever, but since he had been unmasked as a Venator, he looked older. No longer the rebellious youth, but serious and somber in a dark coat and tie.

Several members of the Conclave exchanged raised eyebrows, and white-haired Brooks Stewart had a coughing fit that was severe enough for Cushing Carondolet to pound him on the back several times. When the ruckus subsided, Kingsley continued without comment.

"I bring grave news. There is a disturbance on the South American continent. My team has detected ominous signs that point to a possible *infractio*."

Mimi understood the word from the sacred language—Kingsley was telling telling them of a breaking. But a breaking of what?

"What's been going on?" Dashiell Van Horn wanted to know. Mimi recognized him as the inquisitor during her trial.

"Cracks in the foundation of Corcovado. Some reports of disappearances of Elders of that Conclave. Alfonso Almeida has not returned from his usual sojourn in the Andes. His family is concerned."

Esme Schlumberger snorted. "Alfie just likes to get lost in the wilderness every year. Says it keeps him close to nature. It doesn't mean anything."

"But Corcovado—that is troubling," said Edmund Oelrich, who was now chief warden since Priscilla's death.

"With what we know of the Silver Bloods—how one was able to infiltrate the Repository itself—anything could be possible," Kingsley said.

"Indeed," Dashiell Van Horn agreed, lowering his half-moon spectacles.

Lawrence nodded. "You all know, of course, of the rumors that the Silver Bloods fled to South America before they disappeared. The Blue Bloods kept north, and some believed the Silver Bloods headed south to regroup. Of course, we have never had any evidence of this. . . ."

Several members of the Conclave squirmed visibly. Ever since the attack at the Repository, they had to acknowledge that Lawrence, the former outcast, had been right all along. That the wardens had willfully ignored the signs, had stuck their heads in the sand like a group of ostriches, too fearful to accept the truth: the Silver Bloods, the demons of myth, their ancient foe, had returned.

"We didn't have any evidence until now." Kingsley nodded. "But it looks as though Lawrence's suspicions were correct."

"If Corcovado is compromised, I cannot stress how grave a danger we are in," Lawrence said.

"But there have been no . . . deaths?" asked Eliza Dupont in a timid voice.

"None that we know of," Kingsley confirmed. "One of the young, a Yana Riberio, has also been missing. But her mother thinks she has absconded with her boyfriend on an impromptu weekend in Punta del Este," he said with a smirk.

Mimi kept silent; she was the only member who had yet to contribute to the discussion. In New York, there had been no deaths or attacks since the night at the Repository. She felt frustrated that she couldn't remember why Corcovado was so important—obviously everyone else on the Conclave knew why, but she didn't. It was annoying not to have come into her full memories.

The word meant absolutely nothing to her. And she would never ask anyone what it meant either—she had way too much pride. Maybe she could get Charles to illuminate her, although it seemed that ever since his resignation from the Conclave he had little interest in anything save sitting in his room, poring over old books and photographs, and listening to muffled recordings on an old eight-track.

"As the attack on the Repository has shown, the Silver Bloods are no longer a myth we can choose to ignore. We must act quickly. Corcovado *must* hold," Lawrence declared.

What on earth was Lawrence talking about? Mimi wished she knew.

"So. What is the plan?" Edmund inquired. The atmosphere had shifted. Distress at Kingsley's presence had transformed into distress at the news he had brought.

Kingsley shuffled the papers in front of him. "I'll be joining my team in the capital. São Paolo is a rats' nest. It will make a good hiding place. Then we'll make for Rio on foot, check out the situation in Corcovado, talk to some of the families."

Lawrence nodded. Mimi thought he was going to dismiss the meeting, but he didn't. Instead he removed a cigar from his shirt pocket. Kingsley leaned forward with a lit match, and Lawrence inhaled deeply. Smoke filled the air. Mimi wanted to wave her hands and remind Lawrence of the Committee's no-smoking rule, but she didn't dare.

The Regis regarded the table with a stern eye. "I am

aware that some of you are wondering why Kingsley is here today," Lawrence said, finally addressing the question burning in everyone's mind.

He took another puff from his cigar. "Especially concerning the evidence shown at the blood trial. However, I have since learned that the Martins, and Kingsley in particular, are innocent. Their actions were justified by the mission they were given by the former Regis. For the protection of the Coven, I cannot disclose any more information about this."

Her father! Charles had something to do with it—but why wouldn't Lawrence tell them what it was?

"What mission?" Edmund demanded. "Why was the Conclave kept in the dark about this?"

"It is not our place to question the Regis," Forsyth Llewellyn reminded sharply.

Nan Cutler nodded. "It is not our way."

Mimi could see the table was neatly divided in two: half the members were indignant and anxious, while the other half were prepared to accept Lawrence's statement with no question. Not that it mattered. The Conclave was not a democracy; the Regis was an undisputed leader whose word was law. Mimi trembled with barely suppressed rage. What happened to the Conclave that had condemned her to burn just a few months ago? It wasn't fair! How could they trust a "reformed" Silver Blood?

"Would anyone care to formerly lodge a dissent?" Lawrence asked casually. "Edmund? Dashiell?"

Dashiell bowed his head. "No. We have put our faith in you, Lawrence."

Edmund gave a grudging nod.

"Thank you. Kingsley is once again a voting member of the Conclave, with full Venator status. Join me in welcoming him back to the fold. Without Kingsley, we would not have known about Corcovado so early."

There was a smattering of applause.

The meeting adjourned, and the Elders divided into whispering groups. Mimi noticed Lawrence talking in hushed tones with Nan Cutler.

Kingsley walked up to Mimi and put a light hand on her elbow. "I wanted to tell you that I'm sorry about what happened. The trial and all."

"You set me up," she hissed, shaking off his arm.

"It was inevitable. Still, I'm glad to see you're well," he said. But his tone of voice indicated that her well-being didn't matter to him in the slightest.

The boy stepped into the light, his face illuminated by the fire. He looked the same—the same sad eyes, the same mess of black hair. He was wearing the same dirty T-shirt and jeans that Schuyler remembered him wearing the last time she'd seen him.

"Dylan! But how? What happened? Where have you been?" She ran to hug him, an ecstatic smile on her face. Dylan! Alive! He was not expected, but he was very welcome. She had so many questions to ask him: what happened the night he disappeared? How had he escaped from the Silver Bloods? How was it possible that he survived?

Yet as soon she got close to him, she realized something was very wrong. Dylan's face was grim, angry. His eyes were unfocused and bordering on hysteria.

"What's going on?"

Lightning-fast, Dylan pushed Schuyler with his mind, a

telepathic shove—*SLAM!*—but Schyler was faster and ducked the mind-blow.

"Dylan! What are you doing?!" She held up her hands as if to shield herself, as though she could protect herself with a physical barrier.

SLAM! Another one. This time the suggestion was to throw herself off the balcony.

Schuyler choked, her brain feeling like it might explode from the pressure it was fighting.

She fled to the terrace, not able to stop the suggestion from taking over her senses. She looked over her shoulder. Dylan was right behind her. He looked manic and cruel, as if possessed by some malicious force.

"Why are you doing this?" she cried, as he sent yet another wrenching, agonizing command.

JUMP!

Yes. She must comply, she must obey—JUMP!—yes, she will, but if she is not careful, and she has no time to be . . . she could lose her footing . . . she could . . . Oh God, what if Lawrence is wrong? What if she isn't immortal? She is half human after all . . . What if she doesn't survive? What if, unlike the other Blue Bloods, the cycle of sleep and rest and reincarnation doesn't pertain to her. What if this one life is all she has? But it is much too late to worry about that now—she has no choice. JUMP! She can't see where she's going, she is flailing and scrabbling for purchase . . . He's right behind her, so she's going to . . .

She leaps from the terrace, flying. . . .

No time, no time to scramble for another ledge, no time to grasp a rail . . . The sidewalk looming . . .

Schuyler braced herself for impact and landed on her feet. On her boots. *THUD*. Right into the middle of a stylish mob huddled in front of the Perry St. restaurant. New Yorkers abandoned to the elements because they smoked.

And in a flash, Dylan was right behind her. So fast, he was so very fast. . . .

Then a powerful coercion took over: this was no mere suggestion—this was a control-lock. Crushing. This was what Lawrence had told her was the little-known fifth factor of the glom. The *Consummo Alienari*. Complete loss of one's mind to another.

For the Red Bloods, *alienari* meant instant death. For the vampires, it wrought irrevocable paralysis—the mind taken over so that one's will was completely subsumed. Lawrence had told her that taking the blood and the memories of fellow vampires, performing the *Caerimonia Osculor* on their own kind, was not the only thing Silver Bloods were known for. They had many other tortures and tricks up their sleeve. They did not drain all of their victims; some of them were left to live because they were more useful to the Silver Bloods as pawns.

Schuyler felt a heaviness as the force of the *alienari* settled in . . . she was about to succumb; so much easier to surrender rather than to fight . . . she felt herself weakening under its hold. . . . What would be left of her if he succeeded? She thought of her mother, alive but not alive, would that be her fate? She was woozy on her feet, swaying; it would be over soon. But then she found something in the dark effluvium—like a tail, the tail of the glom—and she was able to isolate the signal, able to figure out which part was trying to control her, and she twisted it around, like wrestling an alligator—flipped it on its head—and soon she was taking over, and she was bending it to her will, and—

Dylan is screaming—he is the one in pain—he is the one backed up against the wall, unable to move while her mind holds his in her grasp. She can feel it, can feel her dominance taking over, greedily exulting over its triumph. She is squeezing him—his entire being—with her mind. It is like a vise—

She is killing him. . . .

Soon he will no longer be himself . . . but an extension of her will. . . .

Until . . .

"SCHUYLER! STOP!"

"DON'T!"

"SCHUYLER!" A roar.

Her name. Someone was calling her name. Oliver. Telling her to stop.

Schuyler released her hold, but not completely. She was still holding out her hand, and twenty feet away, Dylan was pinned to a wall. Held there by her mind. He was gurgling. He couldn't breathe.

"PLEASE!" It was a girl's voice this time. Bliss.

There. She let go.

Dylan sagged to the ground.

*B*liss ran as fast as she could. She had seen the whole thing. She was in the cab and she'd seen it all: Schuyler's jump, Dylan coming after, the chase, the reversal. She'd witnessed Dylan's anguish and Schuyler's mastery.

Oh God, don't let her have killed him.

"Dylan!" Bliss kneeled by his side. He lay facedown on the sidewalk, so she turned him over gently and took him in her arms. He was so thin . . . just skin and bones underneath a T-shirt. She held him tenderly like a baby bird. He was damaged and pathetic, but he was hers. Tears streamed down her cheeks. "Dylan!"

When she'd arrived home after her go-see appointment and he wasn't there to meet her as they'd planned, she'd known immediately that something was wrong. She called Oliver and told him to meet her at the Perry Street apartment building as soon as he could. Dylan had been saying all along he was going to do something, and now he had. Luckily, Bliss knew where to find him because she knew Schuyler's secret and where she was going to be that night.

Dylan opened his eyes. He recoiled when he saw Bliss, and then turned to Schuyler and snarled in a deep, booming rumble, *"Argento Croatus!"*

"Are you insane?" Schuyler asked, Oliver standing by protectively. She couldn't believe her ears. Dylan had just called her a Silver Blood. What was going on? What had happened to him? Why did his voice sound like that?

"Dylan, stop it. Sky—he doesn't know what he's talking about," Bliss said nervously. "Dylan, please, you're not making sense."

Dylan spaced out, his pupils dilating rapidly as if a flashlight were shining in his eyes. Then he started laughing in a high-pitched squeal.

"You've known he was back and you didn't tell me," Schuyler said, and the accusation hung in the air between them.

"Yes." Bliss took a sharp breath. "I didn't want to tell you because . . ." *Because you would tell the Conclave. You would have them take him away. And yes, he's changed. He's different. He's not the same. Something awful and unspeakable has happened to him. But I still love him. You understand, don't you? You, who wait in an apartment for a boy who does not arrive.*

Schuyler nodded. The two of them understood each other without speaking. It was the vampire way.

"Still, he can't be like this; we've got to get him help." Schuyler moved closer to the two of them.

"Don't touch me," Dylan snarled. Suddenly, he leaped to his feet and grabbed Bliss by the throat, his bony fingers pressing violently on her pale neck.

"If you're not going to help me, then you're one of them," he said menacingly, tightening his grip.

Bliss began to cry. "Dylan . . . don't."

Schuyler lunged toward Dylan, but Oliver restrained her. "Wait," he said. "Wait—I can't let you get hurt again. . . ."

Meanwhile, Dylan pushed Bliss further and further with his mind, his fury relentless, his power only more frightening in its recklessness. Bliss dropped to her knees. There would be no telepathic gymnastics on her part.

Now it was Schuyler's turn to scream. Schuyler's turn to beg him to stop.

Dylan took no notice of them, and stroked Bliss's cheek with his other hand. He leaned in, his mouth on her neck. Schuyler could see his fangs appear. They were about to draw blood.

"No . . . Dylan . . . please," Bliss whispered. "No . . ."

"Let me go." Schuyler shook Oliver off her. Bliss watched as her friend frantically prepared an incantation that would break Dylan's hold.

But just before Schuyler could send the coercion, Dylan's shoulders shook and he sank to the ground of his own volition, abruptly releasing his victim. Bliss crumpled to the floor, violet imprints from his fingers blooming on her neck.

Dylan put his head between his knees and sobbed.

"What the hell just happened?" he cried, and finally his was a voice Bliss recognized. For the first time that evening, Dylan sounded like himself.

EIGHT

"Try it," Mimi said, holding a spoon on which a gelatinous mound quivered. "It's delicious."

Her brother looked suspiciously at the appetizer. Gelée of sea urchin with foamed asparagus did not sound good. But he took a bite manfully.

"See?" Mimi smiled.

"Not bad." Jack nodded. She was right as always.

They were seated in a private banquette in a restaurant located in the gleaming Time Warner Center. A restaurant that was, for the time being, the most expensive and most celebrated restaurant in Manhattan. Getting a reservation at Per Se was akin to getting an audience with the pope. Near impossible. But that's what Daddy's secretaries were for.

Mimi liked the new mall, as she called it. It was shiny and glossy and slick, just like the Force Tower. It smelled thrillingly expensive, like a new Mercedes. The building and everything in it was a paean to capitalism and money. You couldn't spend less than five hundred dollars for a meal for two at any of its four-star restaurants. This was post-boom, seven-figure-bonus New York, the New York of financiers and ready-made billionaires, the New York of brash hedge-fund jockeys with shellacked trophy wives flaunting their liposculpted physiques and couture hair extensions.

Jack, of course, hated it. Jack preferred a city that he had never even experienced. He waxed nostalgic about the legendary days of the Village, when anyone from Jackson Pollock to Dylan Thomas could be found wandering the cobblestoned streets. He liked grit and dirt and a Times Square that was known for its hustlers and three-card-monte dealers and underground juice bars (since strip clubs couldn't serve alcohol). He couldn't stomach a New York that had been taken over by the likes of Jamba Juice, Pinkberry, and Cold Stone.

He had been prepared to despise the precious, sixteen-table restaurant in the middle of what was essentially a shopping mall. But as each course appeared—caviar and oyster sabayon, white truffles generously grated over slippery tagliatelle noodles, marrow over the richest Kobe beef—Mimi could see he was beginning to change his mind. Each dish consisted of a mere handful of bites, just enough to excite the senses and leave them panting for the next gourmet fix.

They had walked in that evening to find the place crawling with Blue Bloods, which was somewhat unexpected since vampires only ate to amuse themselves; but apparently even those who did not need sustenance appreciated having their taste buds tickled. A couple of Elders, emeritus members of the Conclave—Margery and Ambrose Barlow—occupied a corner table. Mimi saw that Margery had fallen asleep again, as she had between each course. But the waiter, who looked like he was used to it by now, simply shook her awake each time he delivered something new to their table.

"So how was the meeting?" Jack asked casually, putting down the spoon and nodding to the busboy that he was done.

"Interesting," she said, taking a sip from her wineglass. "Kingsley Martin's back."

Jack looked surprised. "But he . . ."

"I know." Mimi shrugged. "Lawrence wouldn't explain. Apparently there's a reason, but it's much too important to share with the Conclave. I swear, he runs that thing like it's the seventeenth century. It's a farce having 'voting members.' He doesn't ask our opinion on anything. He just does what he wants."

"He must have good reason for it," Jack said, his eyes lighting up as the waiter brought new delectables. He looked disappointed to find it was just a dollop of potato salad.

Mimi frowned as well. She was expecting gastronomic fireworks, not a picnic dish. But one bite changed her mind. "This is . . . the . . . best potato salad . . . in the world."

Jack agreed, as he busily devoured his.

"This is nice, isn't it?" Mimi said, indicating the room and the view of Central Park. She reached across the table and took his hand.

Almost getting killed in Venice was probably the best thing to have happened to their relationship. Faced with the prospect of losing his twin forever, Jack became the soul of devotion.

She still remembered how he'd held her the night after the Blood Trial. His face had aged overnight with worry. "I was so afraid. I was so afraid of losing you."

Mimi had been moved enough to forgive his transgressions. "Never, my love. We will be together always."

After that, there had been no more talk of Schuyler. Even when the little rat had moved into their home, Jack remained cold and indifferent. He never spoke to her, he barely even looked at her. As far as Mimi could tell, secretly probing his mind when his guard was down, he never thought about Schuyler at all. She was simply an irritating houseguest. Like a blemish you couldn't erase.

Maybe she had accomplished what she'd wanted after all. She hadn't been able to get rid of Schuyler, but the attack had succeeded in securing the love of her vampire twin.

"Butter-poached lobster," the waiter murmured, silently setting down two new dishes.

"So I was thinking, we might as well invite everyone to the bonding," Mimi said, in between bites.

Jack grunted.

"Oh, I know. You like the old-fashioned way, just the two of us in the moonlight, blah, blah, blah. But remember Newport? Now that was a party. And you know, having the Four Hundred at a bonding is the way to go now. I heard Daisy Van Horn and Toby Abeville just got bonded in Bali. It was a 'destination bonding.' " Mimi tittered.

Jack signaled the waiter for another bottle of wine. "You know, most Red Bloods these days wait until their thirties to wed. What's the rush?" he asked, regarding with supreme satisfaction the seventh—or was it eighth?—course: a bowl of chilled pea soup.

"Well, my blood is blue, my friend." Mimi curled her lip. True, the Red Bloods they knew did wait a ridiculously long time for their bondings, but those were mere earthly weddings. Humans broke their vows every day with no consequence. This was a celestial situation. While it was tradition for vampire twins to bond on their twenty-first birthday, Mimi saw no reason to wait until then, and there was nothing in the Code that said they couldn't do it earlier. The sooner they said their vows, the better.

When the oaths were exchanged, their souls would mold to each other. Nothing could come between them. They would become one in this lifetime, as they had in all their others. Once the bond was sealed, it could not be broken for the cycle. Schuyler would become nothing more than a distant memory. Jack would forget whatever feelings he had for her. The bond worked in mysterious and irrevocable ways.

Mimi had seen it in lifetimes before—how her twin would pine for Gabrielle (who was now Allegra Van Alen in this cycle) in his youth, but once he said his vows, he would not even remember her name. Azrael would be the only dark star in his universe.

"Shouldn't we graduate from high school first?" Jack asked.

Mimi didn't listen. She was already planning to get fitted for her bonding dress. "Or I don't know, maybe we could elope to Mexico, what do you think?"

Jack smiled, and continued to eat his soup.

NINE

It occurred to Schuyler that the last time she was at the Odeon, she had been with Oliver and Dylan. It was just over a year ago—Dylan had recently transferred to Duchesne, and Oliver's driver had taken them downtown. They had wandered the streets, in and out of shops and bookstores and record stores, poking in apothecary jars and getting their palms read by a gypsy woman on the sidewalk. Then at the end of the day, they'd trooped into the restaurant, into one of the comfortable, cracked-leather red booths and had eaten *moules frites* while Dylan ordered beers with his fake ID and told them stories about being kicked out of every prep school in the northeast corridor.

Dylan was telling them a new story now, Bliss sitting quietly by his side.

He was telling them about what had happened to him.

Now that he wasn't trying to kill her, Dylan didn't seem

so scary, so . . . crazy and unfocused. Now he just looked too thin, like a cat left out in the rain while its owners were on vacation. His eyes were hooded, and there were black bruises on his cheeks. His skin looked jaundiced and he had cuts—little cuts everywhere on his forearms, as if he'd walked through glass. Maybe he had.

Oliver put an arm around Schuyler. After what just happened, he had gone beyond caring who would see them together. And for once Schuyler agreed. She liked his hand there. Liked feeling protected. Her mind drifted to the empty apartment on Perry Street. But she made herself focus on Dylan.

"I don't remember much, really. I ran away, you know. I went to the old Ward House, on Shelter Island . . . I took some refuge there. But the beast caught up with me eventually. I don't remember much of what happened, but I managed to get away again, and this time I got some help.

"Venators," he continued in an awed tone. "You know about them, right?"

They nodded. They also knew that one had been sent to Duchesne. Bliss told them about how Kingsley Martin was back. Her father had been at the Conclave meeting that afternoon. But Schuyler didn't pay attention to the news; she wanted to know what had happened to Dylan.

"Anyway, they let me stay with them, they took care of me while I was recuperating. One of the SB's got me pretty bad in the neck. But the Venators said it was all right, that I hadn't been 'corrupted,' you know . . . 'turned' into one of them. Anyway"—he looked at Schuyler warily—"I overheard their conversations . . . how the Conclave had finally discovered who was the Silver Blood among us, and they said—"

"They said it was me, didn't they?" Schuyler asked, taking a french fry off Oliver's plate.

Dylan didn't deny it. "They said it was you, that you were the one. The night at The Bank. The last thing I remember was hanging out with you, Schuyler, and they said you were the one who'd attacked me."

"Do you believe that?" she asked.

"I don't know what to believe."

"Do you even know who she is?" Oliver demanded. "I mean, I'm glad you're back and all, man, but you're talking smack. Schuyler is . . . Her mom is . . ." Oliver was so angry he couldn't finish.

"Do you know the story of Gabrielle?" Schuyler asked.

"A little," Dylan admitted. "Gabrielle, the Uncorrupted, who was bonded to Michael, Pure of Heart. The only vampires who didn't sin against the almighty. In this cycle, Michael's name is Charles Force. So what?"

"Gabrielle is my mother," she told him.

"Show him," Bliss urged.

Schuyler pushed the large man's watch she wore on her right wrist. Pushed it up the same way she'd seen Charles do it the night she had accused him of being the Silver Blood.

How funny that now she had to resort to clearing her name in exactly the same way.

Etched in her skin, just like on Charles's, was the mark. It was raised, as if burned there, a sigil. A sword piercing clouds.

"What is it?" Dylan asked.

"The mark of the Archangel," Oliver explained. "She's a Daughter of the Light. There is no way she's a Silver Blood. She's the opposite. She's what they fear."

Schuyler touched the mark. It had always been there, since she was born. She'd thought it simply an odd birth-mark, until Lawrence had pointed it out.

Dylan stared at the mark. It shone. He crossed himself. He looked down at his plate of steak frites. "Then who were they—the Venators who helped me?" he asked, his voice hoarse.

Oliver smiled thinly. He tapped the table in front of his friend. "Isn't it obvious?"

"No."

"I know exactly who they were. They were the Silver Bloods."

DYLAN WARD UPDATE:
Subject has been interrogated and released.

Transcript of interrogation destroyed in accordance
with Regis Mandate 1011.

"Are you sure you'll be okay?" Bliss looked around the dirty hotel room. She'd never been inside. Dylan had always insisted they meet in the lobby of the Chelsea Hotel. The hotel itself had seen better days. It was dilapidated and falling apart, one of the old New York landmarks with a literary and scandalous past. The Chelsea was where a heroin-mad Sid Vicious allegedly stabbed Nancy Spungen, where Dylan Thomas died an alcoholic. It was also the place that inspired Bob Dylan's "Sara" ("Stayin' up for days at the Chelsea Hotel . . .") and where Allen Ginsberg penned some of his poems.

She walked around the room, peering out at the rainy street through the blinds. The first night he had returned to her, she'd been shocked and happy to see him. She'd never truly believed he was gone, but it was still mind-blowing to find out he was alive.

That night she'd begged him to stay nearby, but he had insisted on this hotel. He felt safer downtown he said, and had shuddered at the thought of spending another night in one of those five-star plush hotel suites the Conclave had trapped him in while he was being investigated for Aggie Carondolet's death.

The night he'd returned, she'd wanted to be close to him, to feel his body next to hers. She'd felt a closer kinship to him knowing he was like her, a vampire, than a mere Red Blood she could suck dry. Before he'd left, they'd had . . . not quite a relationship, but more than a flirtation. They'd been about to start something. . . . She still remembered the taste of his skin, the feel of his hands underneath her shirt.

But Dylan hadn't shown any interest in picking up where they'd left off. While he'd never rejected her outright, she still felt rebuffed romantically. That first night, she had tried to put her arms around him, and he'd hugged her impatiently, quickly letting go as if touching her repulsed him. He'd demanded they go seek Schuyler and confront her, and Bliss had spent hours talking him out of his plan. They had argued, and she had marched him to this hotel, where he had been holed up since. . . .

In this dirty, smelly suite. Didn't they have housekeeping? Why was this allowed? Newspapers stacked waist-high, empty cans littered about, ashtrays overflowing with cigarette butts.

"Sorry for the mess."

She took a seat on the corner of a plaid sofa that was covered with the remains of the Sunday *Times*. She suddenly felt so tired. She'd been waiting for him to come back, dreaming about it for so long—and now he was here, but it was nothing at all like she'd imagined. Everything was wrong, wrong, wrong. He had tried to hurt Schuyler; he had tried to hurt *her*.

As if he knew what she was thinking, Dylan spoke. "Bliss, I don't know what came over me back there. You know I would never . . . never . . ."

Bliss nodded curtly. She wanted to believe him, but the strength of his force of will on her mind still throbbed. He had done this to her, cut her with a knife—a mental one, but that did not diminish the sharpness of its blade.

Dylan sat next to her on the couch and pulled her to him. What was he doing? *Now* he wanted to kiss her? *Now* he wanted them to be together? When he'd done nothing but make her believe he didn't want that?

She had to agree with Schuyler and Oliver. Dylan was dangerous. He had changed. Was he corrupted? Was he turning into a Silver Blood? He'd taken Aggie, hadn't he? After their meeting at the Odeon they had placed Dylan in the back of a taxi, and Bliss had had a quick, whispered conference with Sky and Ollie.

"He can't be alone."

"I'll stay with him," she'd promised them.

"Be careful. He's not the same."

"He's not *sane*."

"I know," Bliss admitted.

"What are we going to do?"

"We'll figure it out. We always do." That was Oliver. Always optimistic.

And now here she was, in this dirty, smelly room, with the boy she'd once loved so much her heart had ached for months after his disappearance.

Dylan peeled off his jacket. It was a nylon one, a light beige windbreaker, the kind they sold at warehouse stores where you could buy tires in the same aisle as your underwear. She dimly remembered stuffing a bloody leather jacket in the trash. Whatever happened to that? Incinerated.

She stiffened as his hand grazed her arm lightly.

"What are you doing?" she asked, wanting to be angry but feeling a rushing, queasy excitement instead. He was so different from the Red Blood boys she'd had. Mimi was right—there was something about being with your own kind that got the blood flowing in a different way.

He nuzzled her cheek. "Bliss . . ." The way he said her name, so softly, so intimately, his breath warm in her ear.

"Stay with me," he said. Before she could even halfheartedly protest, he had deftly maneuvered it so they were lying on the couch, her knees underneath his, his thighs pressing against hers, his hands entwined in her hair, and she was running her hands all over his chest—he'd gotten scrawny, but there was a hardness to his muscles that hadn't been there before—then his tongue was in her mouth . . . and it was so sweet. . . . She could feel the tears behind her eyes slipping down her cheek, and he was kissing those away too . . . God, she had missed him . . . He had hurt her, but maybe you only hurt the ones you love?

He fumbled for the hem of her shirt, and she helped him lift it up; he buried his face in the hollow beneath her neck, and then suddenly he jumped away, as if burned.

"You still have that thing," he said, leaning as far back as he could, pressed up against the other end of the couch, away from her. *"Palma Diabolos . . ."* He was speaking in a language she could not understand.

"What?" she asked, still dizzy from his kisses. Still feeling drunk with his scent. She looked at where he was pointing.

The necklace. Lucifer's Bane. The emerald hung in a chain over her heart. Somehow she had never returned it to her father's safe. Somehow she had gotten into the habit of wearing it everywhere.

It comforted her to know it was there. When she touched it, she felt . . . better. Safe. More like herself.

Dylan looked stricken. "I can't kiss you with that thing around your neck."

"What?" Bliss pulled her shirt back over her head.

He continued to look as if he'd been poisoned. "You've been wearing that all along. So that's why I couldn't . . . I knew there was a reason." Then he was babbling again. In a different language. This time it sounded Chinese.

Bliss put her shirt back on. He was *incredible*. She'd been a total idiot. Okay, so maybe she'd promised Schuyler and Oliver she'd keep an eye on him, but it wasn't like he was a danger anymore. He knew Schuyler wasn't a Silver Blood. Plus, he was old enough to take care of himself.

She certainly wasn't going to stay here one second longer. She was humiliated. She had no idea how he really felt about her. He ran hot and cold. One minute he was ripping her clothes off, and the next minute he was cringing away from her as if her body were the most disgusting thing he'd ever seen. She was tired of this game.

"You're leaving?" Dylan asked as she gathered her things and headed toward the door.

"For now."

He gazed at her sadly. "I miss you when you're gone."

Bliss nodded as if he'd just told her something innocuous about the weather. Dylan could take his hangdog eyes and his sexy voice somewhere else. She just wanted to be alone.

ast call, guys," the waitress informed them "Another Campari?" she asked Oliver.

He rattled the ice cubes and emptied his cocktail glass in one gulp. "Sure."

"Anything for you?"

Schuyler considered another glass of Johnnie Walker Black. She used to hate the taste of whiskey but lately had developed a liking for it. It was fiery and sweet and succulent—the closest thing you could get to the taste of blood. Oliver had once asked her to describe what it tasted like, since he didn't see the appeal. To him, blood tasted metallic and faintly sweet. Schuyler explained that vampires tasted blood with a different sense—it was like drinking fire.

Hence, her newfound love of whiskey.

"Sure, why not," she told the waitress. It wasn't like it

was going to get her drunk. Although Oliver looked like he was well on his way. He'd come into the habit of fortifying himself with alcohol whenever they got together. Sure, he wasn't drunk when they were together at school—but those abrupt reunions were so brief it didn't matter. But she noticed whenever they spent a substantial amount of time together, he was always a little buzzed.

The waitress returned with two cocktail glasses filled to the brim. It was way past midnight, and the only people left in the place were groggy-eyed clubkids getting breakfast after a late night spent at velvet-rope champagnalias, or groggy-eyed clubkids getting breakfast before an early-morning stint at after-hours lounges where no alcohol was served and the clientele preferred their highs to be chemical ones.

Oliver sipped his cocktail through a red straw. She found it endearing how he liked sweet things. Oliver hated beer and all the usual trappings of what he called "el jocko-Americano." Somehow the girly drinks made him more manly, in Schuyler's eyes. He wasn't afraid to be himself.

It was so nice to finally hang out with Oliver in public. She couldn't very well sink her fangs into him with other people around. Lately, whenever they were alone, it hovered in the air, an expectation on his part, and Schuyler had missed their easy friendship. She relaxed in his company.

"Why do you drink so much around me?" she asked, trying to keep her voice light.

"I'm offended. You think I'm a lush?"

"A little."

"I don't know." He looked up at the ceiling instead of looking at her directly. "Dude, you scare me sometimes."

Schuyler wanted to laugh. "I scare you?"

"Yeah, you're all—vampire superwoman. You could have really done some damage to him, you know." Oliver grinned, although Schuyler knew he was more troubled than he let on.

"He's fine," she snapped. She didn't really want to dwell on what could have happened back there. She had had Dylan in her grasp. She had felt his mind bowing to hers. Had felt all his memories screaming to be let free. And she had wanted nothing more than to crush all of them—silence all their voices. She'd had it in her power to do so. It was a sobering thought, so she took another sip of her drink.

"He's not fine," Oliver said. "You know we have to tell Lawrence about him, don't you? They'll have to do something about it. He's showing classic signs of corruption. Delusions, hysteria, mania."

A busboy cleared their table and gave them the eye. Schuyler knew they should leave, the staff was ready to go home. But she wanted to linger with Oliver just a while longer. "How do you know all this?"

"I did my reading. You know, the stuff Lawrence told us to look up?"

Right. Schuyler felt guilty. She had been remiss on her vampire lessons. Lawrence had been using Oliver to keep her abreast on her studies. She should be concentrating on refining her strengths, on sharpening her skills, but instead she'd been distracted. The Perry Street apartment . . .

"Do you think Dylan was lying to us?" she asked.

"No, I think he thought he was telling us the truth, as much as he knew. But he's obviously been manipulated." Oliver cracked ice cubes in his mouth. "I don't know if I believe he ever really got away from them. I think they let him go."

Schuyler became silent. They had let him go so that he could finish the job he'd failed at before. Dylan had attacked her—twice—before he'd suddenly disappeared. They'd chosen him because he was close to her, was one of her best friends. She couldn't deny it: someone wanted her killed. She wanted to share this realization with Oliver, but kept it to herself. He worried about her enough.

Oliver glanced at the bill and put down his credit card. "So, how are things over at the Death Star?"

"The same." Schuyler smiled, although she felt sick enough to throw up. It was hard to see Oliver and not hate herself because of what she was doing to him.

"So . . ." Oliver sighed. Schuyler knew where this was going and wished once again that she hadn't made him her familiar.

"So?"

The waitress returned with the credit-card slip and hinted that if they stayed any longer they'd have to leave through the back entrance.

Oliver pocketed his card and tried to take another gulp of his already empty drink. "I was on my way to meet you at the Mercer when Bliss called. She said you were down here, on Perry Street. I thought that was kind of odd, since we'd agreed we'd meet at the Mercer, as usual, but she said she was positive you'd be there. What were you doing in that building anyway?"

Schuyler wouldn't look him in the eye. "Modeling thing. Linda Farnsworth has a place for the models to crash there. Bliss and I go there sometimes to hang out with a couple other girls. I didn't realize the time. I'm sorry I kept you waiting."

"Well, um, since we didn't get to meet like we'd planned, do you want to . . ."

It was easier to rebuff him this time, since she'd already made her decision earlier. Schuyler shook her head. "No, I've got to be back for the curfew. I'm late enough as it is, and if Charles finds out—"

"Fuck Charles." Oliver flicked a toothpick across the table so it landed on the floor. "I mean, God, sometimes I'm so tired of all this shit."

"Ollie—"

"I just want us to be together," he said, looking at the ceiling again. "I mean, I know it's not possible. But why not? Why should we follow the old laws? Why should anyone care anyway?" he railed. "Don't you want us to be together?" he challenged, an edge to his voice.

Schuyler was moved to take his hand in hers. "I do, Ollie, you know I do." He was her ally, her partner-in-crime, her conscience and her comfort.

Oliver's face transformed into a look of utmost happiness and satisfaction. He smiled at her then, and Schuyler hoped with all her heart that he would never find out the truth.

*I*t was late when Mimi and Jack finally wobbled out of Per Se. The bill for their meal was in the four-figure range, not that Mimi was surprised. She was so used to paying exorbitant prices for everything in her life, she sometimes complained when she discovered something was cheaper than she'd expected. "What do they think, that I'm poor?" she sniffed. "That I can't afford FIJI Water?"

Jack chided her for her extravagance. "It's the mistake of the nouveau riche, you know, believing that having a lot of money is the same as having an infinite amount of money."

Mimi stared at him incredulously. "Did you just call me nouveau riche?"

Jack barked a laugh as they got on the elevator. "I guess so."

"Bastard!" Mimi pretended to be terribly offended. "Our money is so old it's drawing social security. Bankruptcy's out of the question. We're flush."

"I hope so. Didn't you say Lawrence reported a huge dip in earnings? And I've listened in on the latest investor appraisals. FNN is down several points. It's not good news."

She faked a big yawn. "Don't bore me with details. I'm not worried."

They walked out into the night. Across the street, horses hitched to hansom cabs awaited clueless tourists. It was cold—the last dredge of winter. Vestiges of the most recent snowstorm remained in the form of yellowy, cracked ice on top of garbage bins and the sidewalks.

Jack raised his hand, and a sleek black Bentley as large as a hearse pulled up to the curb.

"Home?" Mimi asked as she slid into the seat.

Jack leaned over, his arm resting on the edge of the door. "I'll see you there in a bit. I told Bryce and Jamie I'd meet them at the club."

"Oh."

He bussed her cheek. "Don't wait up, okay?" Then he shut the door and rapped smartly on the window. "Take her home, Sully."

Mimi waved at him through the tinted glass, her good mood evaporating as she watched him walk across the street to catch a cab headed downtown.

"Home, Miss Force?" Sully turned around.

She was about to nod. She was tired. Home sounded like a good idea. Though she was a little piqued that she had to go home alone. She toyed with the idea of following him, but

Jack had been so devoted of late . . . There was nothing to suspect . . . He always met Bryce Cutting and Jamie Kip at the club . . . silly boys. And besides, she'd been watching him like a hawk in the past few weeks, ever since Venice, and had felt guilty because she had found nothing. What was she so worried about anyway?

But she had to be honest with herself. She was worried. "Not yet, Sully. Let's see where he's going."

The driver nodded. He'd heard this request before.

"Make sure he doesn't see us."

The car trailed the cab heading south on the West Side Highway. Block 122 had closed, and the new hot club of the moment, the Dante Inn, was located farther downtown, in the West Village, in the basement of one of those new glass buildings right off the highway. Mimi remembered Jack telling her how the family had bought an apartment there, as an investment. The place was currently being rented out to some celebrity.

The cab pulled up to the entrance, a velvet rope hooked between two fire escape railings and guarded by a tall man in a black greatcoat. The Dante Inn was a smaller venue, less flashy than Block 122, but even more exclusive. Jack got out and disappeared inside.

Mimi leaned back happily. "Okay, let's go." She watched as a white limousine drove up in front of them. God, people were so tacky. And Jack was calling *her* nouveau riche?

She tried to see if she could recognize the rowdy people

from the limo—that one had to be a famous actor, because he was wearing a trilby hat like a moron—when she saw something else: someone emerged from the shadows and slipped inside the main doors to the building. A figure in a silver raincoat, with dark hair.

No.

It couldn't be.

It couldn't be Schuyler Van Alen. Could it? Of course it was.

Mimi felt her heart clench. It was too much of coincidence. Jack was in the club that was located in the basement of the same building Schuyler had just entered.

It couldn't be. Her mind raced; had she missed something? But he had been so indifferent, so cold to Schuyler. He couldn't still be infatuated, could he?

He doth protest too much.

Mimi was never a big fan of Shakespeare, not even during his lifetime, but she remembered the important lines. This was definitely the winter of her discontent.

She knew, without having it confirmed, that no matter what kind of front Jack put up to the world, what kind of lies he told her, there was a secret place in his heart that she could not read or fathom. A secret place that was devoted to someone else. A secret place inhabited by Schuyler Van Alen.

Strangely enough, Mimi did not feel betrayed, or stricken, or devastated. She merely felt a heavy sadness. She had tried so hard to help him. She had tried to keep him loyal to her.

How could he act with no fear of reprisal? He knew the laws as well as she. He knew what was at stake. He knew what he could lose.

Oh, Jack. Don't let me have to hurt you. Don't let us be estranged in this way. Don't make me have to hunt you down.

"*I* thought you'd forgotten."

Schuyler smiled as she removed her raincoat and hung it on the hook. She had just entered the apartment with her key. A key she kept on a silk ribbon around her neck. She never took it off, for fear that it would be stolen. She'd entered the building in the normal fashion. Had a polite word with the guard. Headed up in the elevator, exchanging pleasantries with the neighbors. Cooed at their baby bundled inside a fleece-lined thousand-dollar stroller. Pretended she was just like them. No more vampire tricks for one evening.

"Have you been waiting long?" she asked.

"I just got here."

He was standing against a column, his arms crossed in front of him. He was still wearing the same white shirt from that morning, a little crumpled at the end of the day, and he had loosened his tie, letting it fall to the side. But he was still golden and gorgeous. His sea green eyes danced with amusement and desire. Jack Force. The boy she had been waiting to see all evening. The boy she had been waiting for all her life.

She wanted to run to him—to skip, giggling into his arms—but she savored the way he was looking at her. She could drown in the intensity of his gaze. And she had learned a little about seduction in the last few weeks they had been together.

Had learned that it was sweeter when she made him wait.

So she took her time, removed her shoes, brushed her bare feet on the carpet, and let him watch her.

Outside of this place, they could be nothing to each other. He would not even allow himself to look at her. He could not afford it. So she wanted him to enjoy himself, to look at her as much as he liked.

"Get over here," he growled.

And then, at last, she ran—leaped into his arms, and together they crashed against the wall in a tight embrace. He lifted her with graceful ease, covering her body with kisses.

She tightened her legs around his torso and bent over, brushing his cheek with the tendrils of her hair.

Jack.

She felt liquid in his arms. Pressed against him, his heart beating wildly in time with hers. When they kissed, she closed her eyes and saw a million colors bursting in the air, glorious and alive. He smelled earthy and lush, warm and brutish. It had been a surprise: she'd assumed he would smell like ice—like nothing—and she liked that he smelled coarse and real. He was not a dream.

She knew that what they were doing was wrong. Lawrence had warned her that vampire bonds should not be broken. Jack was sworn to another. She had promised herself to stop, but she had also promised Jack she would always be there for him. They were so happy together. They belonged to each other. Yet they never spoke about the past or the future. Only this existed, this little bubble they'd made, this little secret. And who knew how long they had?

When she was in his arms, she felt sorry for Mimi.

It had started right after she'd settled into that palace of gilt and marble the Forces called home. The place was part fortress and part Versailles. There were rooms and ante-rooms filled with magnificent antiques polished and theatri-cally lit on display. Oceans of expensive fabric swathed the windows, and a silent crew of servants moved around the house, dusting, cleaning, offering its occupants tea or coffee on silver service trays.

She had sat on the princess bed in her designated room, kicking at the battered trunk that was the only remnant of home she'd allowed herself to bring. Lawrence had promised that he would get her out somehow, that she would return to her rightful home soon. He knew Charles would not allow him to have contact with her, so they had agreed they would use Oliver as a (she smiled a little) conduit between them.

Lawrence had driven her to the Forces' town house himself. Had helped carry her bags to the front door, where a gloved butler took over. Too soon, her grandfather had left, and Schuyler was alone again.

Charles had given her a quick tour of the house: the sparkling Olympic-size pool in the basement, tennis courts on the roof, the gym, the sauna, the Picasso room (so called because it contained one of the two mural-size black-and-white studies of the masterpiece *Les Demoiselles d'Avignon*). He'd told her to make herself comfortable, to avail herself of everything in the kitchen. Then he'd laid down his rules. Schuyler had been too angry and annoyed to do more than dumbly nod at everything.

So she'd decided to kick her trunk. Stupid trunk. Stupid trunk with the broken lock. Stupid ugly trunk that was one of the few things she'd kept that her mother had owned. It was an old Louis Vuitton traveling valise, the kind that, when stood upright and opened, revealed a mini wardrobe. She kicked it again.

There was a soft knock on the door, and then the door was pushed open.

"Do you think you could . . . um . . . keep it down a bit? I'm trying to read," Jack said, looking bemused.

"Oh! Sorry." She stopped kicking the trunk. She'd wondered when she'd see her *cousins*. The complicated ties of vampire families still eluded her, but she knew that she and Jack weren't technically blood-related, even though Charles was her uncle. Someday she'd have to ask Lawrence how it all shook down. "What are you reading?"

"Camus," he said, holding up a copy of *The Stranger*. "Have you read it?"

"No, but I like The Cure song. You know, the one that's based on that book?"

He shook his head. "Nope."

"I think it's on *Three Imaginary Boys*. Their first album. Robert Smith, he's a big reader too. Probably an existentialist like you," she teased.

Jack leaned against the wall and crossed his arms, regarding her thoughtfully. "You hate it here, don't you?"

"Does it show that much?" Schuyler asked, pulling the long sleeves of her sweater over her hands.

He chuckled. "I'm sorry."

"You're sorry."

He put the book down on a vanity table. "It's not so bad."

"Really? What's good about it?"

"Well, for one, I'm here," he said, coming over to sit next to her on the bed. He picked up a tennis ball that had rolled out of her trunk. She'd brought it to practice her vampire lessons. Lawrence wanted her to concentrate on the ability to move objects in the air, something she had yet to master. Jack threw it in the air, catching it deftly. Then he put it down. "Unless, you know, you want me to go."

He was sitting so close to her. She remembered how she'd run to him the first night she was attacked, how passionate he'd been about discovering the truth about Croatan, and then how deeply he'd disappointed her when he'd brushed her aside. And then she remembered something else. Something she couldn't stop thinking about ever since she'd drawn Mimi's blood and absorbed her memories.

"You were the one—that night of the masquerade ball— it was you who . . ." Schuyler whispered, and in answer to her question, he kissed her. The kiss was the third one they'd exchanged (she kept count), and as he breathed into her and cupped her face in his broad hands, everything in her life up until then seemed secondary and ordinary.

There was nothing to live for but this pure, heavenly sensation. The first time they'd kissed, she had glimpsed Jack's memories of a girl who looked like her but was not her. The second time, she'd had no idea he was the one behind the mask, but this time it was just the two of them. Jack wasn't kissing someone he thought he'd known before, and Schuyler wasn't kissing someone she didn't know. They were simply kissing each other.

"Jaaaack! Jaaaaack!"

"Mimi," Jack said. He disappeared so fast out of the room it was as if he had turned invisible.

When Mimi poked her head into Schuyler's room, she was sitting by herself kicking the trunk again. "Oh. You. Have you seen Jack?"

Schuyler shook her head.

"By the way, don't get too comfortable around here. I have no idea why Father wants a little creep like you around, but here's some advice: keep out of my way."

Later that night, Schuyler had received two different welcome presents: someone had short-sheeted her bed, and there was a book slipped under her door. A copy of *The Plague* by Albert Camus. Inside the book was an envelope, and inside the envelope, there was a key.

From then on, Jack never acknowledged her presence at the house or at school. But he had more than made up for it later.

"Where'd you get this?" Jack asked, tracing a cut on her forehead with a light finger. They were lying on the thick shag carpet, gazing at the remnants of the fire.

"Oh. It's nothing. Banged my head," Schuyler said. She didn't want to tell him about Dylan just yet. "Were you followed?"

"Yes. But I made sure she left before I got here," he said. His voice was sleepy, and she nestled in the crook of his arm. The streetlights were the only light in the room, but she could see him clearly in the dark. His perfect profile, as if sculpted in marble, glowed like a candle. "You?"

"No."

In reality she had not checked. She had been too busy talking Oliver into leaving. Too busy and too excited. Because she had known, hadn't she? She had known Jack would be there, waiting for her, as she had waited for him earlier.

But yes, next time she would be more careful. They would both have to be.

FOURTEEN

Bliss arrived late to the Lexington Armory. The Rolf Morgan show was scheduled to start at nine in the evening, and she was supposed to be there by six for hair and makeup, but it was already half past eight. She hoped the designer wouldn't kill her, although he'd probably already written her off, and she'd arrive to find some other model wearing the black-lace corset dress she was supposed to wear that evening.

She hadn't meant to be late, but her latest vision had left her disoriented. She'd been brushing her teeth, and when she looked up at the mirror, the same handsome man in the white suit from her dreams was looking back at her.

"Jesus!"

"Hardly." The man laughed as if it were the funniest thing he'd ever heard. His hair, Bliss realized, was the exact color of molten gold. His eyes were as blue as a clear morning sky. There was a smell in the room of lilies in the spring, but it was a cloying smell that masked something rotten. Like how her stepmother, BobiAnne, smelled when she put on too much perfume after leaving the gym instead of showering.

Bliss decided she would be brave. "Who are you?"

"I am you."

"I'm going crazy, aren't I? Why are you here?" Bliss turned off the faucet and tried to steady her breathing. "What do you want?"

The golden man in the white suit reached into his coat pocket and removed an old-fashioned pocket watch that hung from a gold chain. "Time."

When Bliss looked up at the mirror again, he was gone. She'd spent the next hour staring at the glass, waiting for him to appear again. Only when she'd finally wrenched herself away did she realize she was running so late.

But when she checked her cell phone, there were no angry messages from her model booker, no anxious harangues about how the designer was having a fit because she wasn't there. She was doubly confused to find the entrance to the show completely empty, save for a few miserable-looking fashion victims shrouded in black, being held behind police sawhorses. This was fashion week?

Where was the mad carnival of editors and photographers, celebrities and stylists, the fashionable and the fashionably distressed, crowded around, elbowing each other, pushing and shoving to get into the Rolf Morgan show? Rolf's show was the biggest ticket of the season and the hardest invitation to score. And yet, here it was, thirty minutes before showtime and there was hardly anyone around.

She found a lone minion, a production assistant wearing a black T-shirt with ROLF MORGAN emblazoned on the chest, and asked to be directed backstage.

The Armory housed the 69th Regiment of the National Guard, and several soldiers in dress uniform saluted her as she entered. The building was cavernous, and encased in glass cabinets lining the walls were hundreds of firearms and munitions. She followed the directions through a grand atrium, a space as large as an airplane hangar, which was set for a runway show. There were rows of bleachers leading up to the ceiling, and a stage had been set up at one end, where a band was tuning up.

During rehearsals, Rolf had explained that the models would walk on a giant runway suspended above the stage, and Bliss looked forward to the challenge.

She entered the makeshift backstage and was flummoxed to find that instead of the usual frenzy of preparation, thrumming with the adrenaline of fear and excitement, the mood was completely relaxed. She found Schuyler reading a magazine in a nearby chair, her hair pulled back into an extreme ponytail high on her head, her face already runway-ready, with dark kohl smudges lining her blue eyes, and her lips painted a pale, rosy gold.

She was glad to see her friend; they had yet to talk about what had happened the other night. Both of them had been avoiding the subject, almost as if they were embarrassed. She hadn't seen Dylan since then, although he had left her enough messages on her phone, asking for forgiveness and beseeching her to visit him. She had deleted them all.

As for Schuyler, since that evening she had floated around Duchesne in a cloud. Bliss knew Schuyler was seeing Jack, and she couldn't help but be jealous of her friend's newfound happiness. Sure, it sucked that they couldn't be out in public together, because of Mimi and all. And yeah, it totally blew that Jack was basically bethrothed to someone else. But still, Bliss could see Schuyler was in love, and her love was returned. It was more than she could say about Dylan and her.

"Where's everybody?" Bliss asked. "There's no one out-side even."

"Oh, hey." Schuyler put down the latest issue of French *Vogue*. "Yeah, it's closed. Show isn't starting until midnight, if we're lucky. They told everyone to go away and come back."

Bliss slumped into a nearby seat. "Are you serious?"

"Is this your first time walking for Rolf?" another model asked, overhearing their conversation. Bliss recognized her as Sabrina Sorboba, the Eastern European giantess, who was the current designer darling.

Bliss nodded.

"He's always late. Last year Brannon Frost actually left

the show without seeing it, she was so annoyed to be kept waiting," Sabrina told them. Brannon Frost was the Blue Blood editor of *Chic*, the most powerful fashion magazine in the world. Brannon snaps her fingers, and suddenly everyone's wardrobe is out of style. Snap! Volume and pouf. Snap! Wasp-waists and skinny pants. Snap! Shifts and round heels! Snap! Crochet and platforms! Snap!

"Midnight? That's in three hours!" Bliss complained. What were they supposed to do, just wait around? She noticed some of the models were playing cards, although most were on their cell phones and BlackBerries.

"Champagne?" Sabrina offered, lifting a magnum of Laurent-Perrier and pouring two glasses for Bliss and Schuyler without waiting for an answer. This was the answer to waiting: drink, smoke, and wait. As a concession to the latest are-models-too-thin scandal, there was a delusory spread of stale crackers and moldy cheese to provide "healthy" foods for the girls. As if! Models lived on fumes: smoke and air.

"Anyway, because of what happened last year, this time they called all the editors of *Chic*, *Mine*, and *Jeune* and told them to go get a drink or dinner and come back later."

Bliss nodded. "So who're those people outside, then?"

"Nobodies."

Figured. Of course all the important people would be warned, but as for the lesser echelons, they had to fend for themselves. She tucked her bag underneath the counter and was about to ask Schuyler a question, when a harried man—finally someone who looked and acted like they had to put on a show in a few hours—burst into the models' waiting room.

"Bliss! There you are. We need you in hair and makeup."

Bliss flipped through the latest issue of *Arena Homme*, smoked a few cigarettes, and drank too much champagne while a curt hairstylist and his equally tense assistant teased and brushed her hair into a huge billowing creation, and a mellow makeup artist slathered on the spackle. It always amazed her how little effort modeling was. All she had to do was sit there. Then she had to stand. Then walk. That was it. Of course, one had to be breathtakingly beautiful to make it all "work." Still, it wasn't enough to be jaw-droppingly gorgeous. The best models had a certain air of languor and mystery that was innate to their personalities. There was only one Kate Moss, after all.

When the beauty team was satisfied with their work, two eager design students, who were part of the large volunteer army that shouldered the actual physical labor and made fashion week happen, accosted her next. "We have to get you into your first outfit. Rolf wants to see it."

The two students helped Bliss into the tight black corset dress. One of them pulled and tied the ribbons in the back while the other helped Bliss into a pair of ankle-length velvet boots that criss-crossed in the front. The dress hugged every curve, and the peekaboo black lace lent the dress a smoky sexiness. The corset bodice dipped so low in the front, Bliss blushed at how much of her skin was exposed.

"What's that?" one of the students asked, pointing to the shining emerald necklace nestled in her cleavage.

"It's mine."

"I don't know if Rolf is going to like it," the other student said hesitantly.

Bliss shrugged. She didn't care what Rolf wanted. She would never take it off.

*A*t exactly five minutes to midnight, Mimi and Jack Force entered the Armory to a torrent of flashbulbs. Mimi leaned on Jack's shoulder, pulling her fluffy zebra-striped sable coat closer and hiding behind a pair of extra-large sunglasses, as if the excess of photography could harm her.

"Watch it," Jack said sharply to an overeager paparazzo who came a little too close and jostled Mimi.

"Mimi! Right here," a young publicist wearing a headset said, sweeping them into the main room and leading them quickly through the fashionista sea to the very first row. "We're a minute to go-time. You're here next to Brannon."

The room buzzed with excitement, every seat in the house was full, every celebrity was accounted for (Mimi was one of the last), and even the aisles were full of the black T-shirt-wearing volunteers who crept out from backstage and into the main room to watch the action. Onstage, the band thundered through a raucous alt-rock anthem.

Mimi preened for the cameras, shrugging off her fur coat and flexing her calves so that her legs would look thinner. She had no envy for the models; they would only be photographed for the clothes on their backs. Whereas the dizzying crowd surrounding her and yelling her name were taking her picture because they were interested in *her*.

"You're really enjoying this," Jack teased.

"Mmmm." For the past week she had concealed her rage so well she thought she deserved an Oscar. But she couldn't even bear to look at her twin. That liar, that traitor. He was risking everything for a dalliance with the half-blood mongrel. She could see through his solicitousness and realized how well he had snowed her for so long. The bastard was only pretending to be in love with her, while he concealed his real feelings.

The worst part of it all was that she couldn't even hate him. She loved him too much and understood his flaws too well. Hating Jack would be akin to hating herself, and Mimi had too much self-esteem to wallow in that particular misery.

"Mimi! Darling!" Randy Morgan, the designer's wife, suddenly swooped down upon them and effusively kissed her on both cheeks. "You must come backstage and wish Rolf good luck!"

Mimi allowed herself to be led to the traditional bow-and-scrape with the designer. The designer, of course, would be the one doing the bowing and scraping. Mimi was one of his biggest clients.

She left Jack and picked her way through the crowd. Rolf greeted her with a bear hug and a shower of compliments. Mimi accepted the homage and generously wished him a good show. She said hello to several other Blue Bloods from her social circle: Piper Crandall in an atrocious yellow dress, and Soos Kemble, who complained about being relegated to the second row. Mimi spied a few uppity Red Bloods as well. Lucy Forbes cooed over Mimi's new Rolf Morgan ensemble that the designer had messengered over just that morning for her to wear to his show. Then she spied the object of her hatred across the room.

Schuyler was letting her dressers fuss over her outfit: a ruffled blouse and a slim-cut riding jacket, velveteen riding pants and high boots. Mimi thought to herself she would buy the outfit if Schuyler weren't the one wearing it.

Without hesitation she walked over to Schuyler. Maybe she could nip this thing in the bud; maybe there was still hope that nothing would come of Jack's stupid little flirtation.

"Schuyler, you have a second?" she asked.

Schuyler sent her handlers away, and the two of them drifted over to a quiet corner. "What's up?"

Mimi decided to get right to the point. "I know what's going on between you and my brother."

"What do you mean?" Schuyler tried to look calm, but Mimi could sense her alarm. She was right. Goddamnit she was right. The wretch didn't even try to deny it. The two of them were together. How far had it gone? Mimi's heart dropped. She had told herself she would never feel jealous of the annoying little mutt. But Schuyler's defiant face made her feel otherwise.

Schuyler didn't look chastened, or weak, or embarrassed. Gone was the whimpering half-blood who jumped when you said "Boo!" Gone was the girl with the unrequited crush on the great Jack Force. Mimi saw Schuyler very clearly. She looked like a girl who was confident in love. A girl who knew she held his heart in her hands. For a moment Mimi intensely wished the Silver Blood had dragged Schuyler face-down into hell.

"Do you have any idea what you're doing to Jack?"

"What are you talking about?"

Mimi clutched Schuyler's upper arm tightly. "Think of your mother. Why do you think Allegra's in a coma? Why do you think she's immortal but won't die? She is useless and destroyed. Do you want that for him?"

"Don't bring my mother into this," Schuyler warned, shaking Mimi off. "You don't know anything about my mother."

"Oh, but I do. I have lived much longer than you." Mimi's face changed, and for a moment, Schuyler saw flashes of all the women in history Mimi had been: the Egyptian queen, the French noblewoman, the hardy Pilgrim, the Newport hostess—all breathtakingly beautiful, all with the same cold green eyes.

"You don't understand the bond," Mimi whispered, as around them the designer and his team were making final corrections on all the clothes. "Jack and I are one and the same. Taking him away from me would be like ripping off his skin. He needs me. If he renews the bond, he will grow stronger, his memories will be whole. He will flourish."

"And if not?" Schuyler challenged.

"You might as well reserve a spot for him in that hospital my father keeps visiting. This is not some silly high school game, you stupid girl." This is life and death. Angels and demons. The bond is law. We are made from the same dark matter, Mimi thought but didn't say. She saw that Schuyler could not, or would not, understand. Schuyler was a newborn. She had no comprehension of the rigors of immortality. The harsh and absolute ways of their kind.

"I don't believe you."

"I didn't expect you to." Mimi looked exhausted. "But if you do love him, leave him, Schuyler. Release him. Tell him you don't want him anymore. It's the only way he'll let go."

Schuyler shook her head. Around her, the models were lining up, and Rolf was pinning a hem here, tucking in a pleat there. Outside, the lights had gone black and the show was about to start. She let one of her dressers snip an errant thread from the sleeve of her riding jacket. "I can't do that. I can't lie."

Mimi took a sip from Schuyler's glass of champagne without asking. "Then Jack is lost."

Sixteen

*L*ast year during his fall presentation, Rolf Morgan had made the audience walk down the runway while the models sat on front-row seats and pretended to take notes. The gimmick had charmed the fashion press so much he was keen on trying out another fun twist. This year the show would be run backward, starting with the designer's bow and the grand ball gowns and ending with casual sportswear.

As the band played a thundering rendition of "Space Oddity," Rolf ran out onto the stage to thunderous applause. He returned bearing a bouquet of roses, beaming and energized. Schuyler watched as Cyrus, Rolf's spastic show runner, led Bliss to the front of the line. The black lace corset dress was meant to be the showstopping finale, and therefore, in the backward equation, the opener. Schuyler gave Bliss an encouraging wave. She knew her friend was still slightly intimidated by the catwalk, and Bliss looked like a nervous colt, her hands quivering slightly as they rested on her hips.

Bliss returned a few minutes later, a broad smile of relief on her face. "It's madness out there!" she gushed to Schuyler before being whisked away to get changed for her second outing.

Schuyler returned Bliss's smile, thinking she would be glad when it was over, when she could finally put on her own clothes—a certain men's Oxford shirt that was her current favorite, over a pair of black leggings and cloven-hoof boots that she'd picked up at a resale shop.

The girls in their gothic prom dresses had exited the catwalk, and Cyrus motioned her to the front. She was next. "Remember, when you get to the end, one pose, two pose, BAM! And then come back."

Schyler nodded. She took a deep breath and walked onstage. Stepping out onto the catwalk was like stepping onto the moon. You went from the grungy reality of backstage, surrounded by chatter and safety pins and a heroic mess of clothing racks and raided accessory bins, to the bright white lights of the stage and the blinding flash of a hundred cameras.

The atmosphere was electric, a noisy cacophony of hysteria reserved for the best rock concerts—the hoots and cheers from the back row energizing the band to play faster and louder, and the models to assume their haughtiest facades. Schuyler never even noticed the grim-faced editors or the tarted-up celebrities in the front row; she was too busy concentrating on putting one foot in front of the other and not making a fool of herself.

She found the marked spot at the end of the runway and snapped the required poses, turning left and rotating her hip forward, and turning right soon after. And just as she was about to do an about-face to turn back, her mind opened to an urgent, forcible sending. It was an incoherent, savage hatred. The unexpected intensity was enough to stop Schuyler in mid-step, and she staggered from the weight of it, tripping over her heels and causing members of the front row to gasp audibly.

Schuyler felt disoriented and broken. Someone—or something—had savagely entered her mind. She recognized it immediately as a manipulation, but this was stronger and more evil than what she had experienced with Dylan. It was an unforgivable trespass, and she felt violated, naked, and terribly afraid. She had to get out of there.

There was no time to make a proper exit. Schuyler leaped from the stage, landing in the middle of the photographer's pit. She knew exactly where she had to go now.

"Sorry!" she told one unlucky shutterbug whose foot she had crushed.

She flew through the crowd, to the confusion of the crew and the delight of everyone else, who thought it was all part of the show.

From backstage she heard, "Hey! Where does she think she's going? Get back here!"

Tomorrow there would be a tabloid story about the model who had run off the catwalk at the Rolf Morgan show, but Schuyler wasn't worried about the media or her model booker or Rolf right then.

What was that? she thought, her heart feeling as if it would explode from fear as she ran up the West Side Highway, moving faster than traffic would ever allow. *Who was that?* The sickly, defiled feeling diminished slightly the moment she arrived at the shabby old brownstone on Riverside Drive. It didn't look as run-down as it used to, thanks to Lawrence's recent renovation. Its stone steps were newly swept, the graffiti on the doors had been painted over, and the gargoyles had been restored to their former dignity.

When she entered her grandfather's study he was bent over, packing a file of papers into a leather attaché case. He had aged in the month they had been separated, Schuyler noticed. His leonine hair was streaked with gray, and there were new lines around his eyes.

Lawrence was an Enmortal, a rare vampire who did not rest, did not go through the regular cycle of reincarnation. He had kept his same physical shell for centuries. He had the ability to look as young as Schuyler, but that evening he looked as if he carried the weight of a thousand years. He looked, for the first time since Schuyler knew him, *ancient*. He did not look like a man from the twenty-first century. He looked as if he had been there when Moses had been put in a basket and sent down the river.

"Schuyler, what a pleasant surprise," he said, although he didn't look surprised to see her.

"Where are you going?" she asked in response, when she saw his battered valise strapped and packed, next to the desk.

"Rio," he said. "There's been a massive earthquake; have you seen the news?" Lawrence asked, motioning to the television that had recently been installed in his office. The cameras showed a city engulfed in flames, entire buildings collapsed into piles of debris.

Schuyler said a quick prayer at the sight of the devastation. "Grandfather, something happened to me. Just a few minutes ago." She described the sensation, the feeling that she was in the presence of an incredible malice. It was only for the briefest moment, but it was enough to feel polluted in every pore of her being.

"So you felt it too."

"What was it?" Schuyler shuddered. "It was . . . repulsive," she said, even though repulsive was too weak a word for the inchoate hostility she had experienced.

Lawrence motioned for her to take a seat while he continued to look through his papers. "In your reading, have you come across the chapter on Corcovado yet?"

"I know it's in Rio. . . . In Brazil," she said hesitantly. She hadn't made much headway on Lawrence's assignments. It was silly of her, but she felt her grandfather was partly to blame for her living situation, and in petulance she had dismissed his suggestions to brush up on her Blue Blood history. He had pressed her to read copies of ancient, formerly forbidden texts—the history of Croatan that had been expunged from the official records until now.

If Lawrence was annoyed, he didn't show it. Instead he explained patiently, like the university professor he had once been. "Corcovado is a place of power, a source of energy, a primal *bivio* from which we vampires draw our strength on Earth. Our immortality stems from a harmonic connection to the primordial essence of life, a gift we have retained even after our banishment."

On screen, the camera showed the famous statue of Christ the Redeemer looming over the city on its pedestal on Corcovado Mountain. Schuyler marveled that it was still standing while buildings all around the city had been reduced to rubble.

"The earthquake. The sending I experienced. It's connected, isn't it? Is that why you're going?" she asked, knowing she was right.

Her grandfather nodded but would not elaborate further. "It is best if you do not know exactly how."

"You're leaving tonight, I take it?" Schuyler asked.

Lawrence nodded. "I'll meet up with Kingsley's team in Sao Paolo first. Then we head to Corcovado together."

"And the Conclave?"

"They are understandably concerned, but it is best if

they do not know too many details of my trip. You know my doubts about the Conclave, what Cordelia and I always suspected."

"That one of the great families has betrayed us," Schuyler said, watching as her grandfather meticulously arranged his necktie. Lawrence always dressed formally for every occasion.

"Yes. But I do not know how. And I do not know why. Of course, our misgivings have never been confirmed, and certainly we have never had any evidence of such a betrayal. Yet the latest attacks confirmed that somehow, one or more of the Silver Bloods survived, and have returned to prey on us. That perhaps the Dark Prince himself still walks this earth."

Schuyler shuddered. Whenever Lawrence spoke about Lucifer, she felt as if her blood had turned to ice. There was evil embedded even in his name.

"Now, Schuyler, I must bid you good-bye."

"No! Let me come with you," Schuyler said, rising from her seat. That dark, terrible, hateful animosity. Her grandfather couldn't face that thing—whatever it was—alone.

"I am sorry." Lawrence shook his head and slipped his wallet into his coat pocket. "You must stay here. You are strong, Schuyler, but you are very young. And you are still under my care."

He drew the blinds and put on an old raincoat. Anderson, his Conduit, appeared at the door. "Ready, sir?"

Lawrence picked up his bags. "Do not look so disappointed, granddaughter. It is not only for your sake that you must remain in New York. If there is one thing I can do for your mother, it's keep you safe from harm, and as far away from Corcovado as possible."

<<Muffled recording. Two distinct voices are heard: Venator Martin and Charles Force, Regis.>>

Venator Martin: She has taken the bait.

Charles Force: Are you perfectly sure?

VM: Yes. There is no doubt in my mind that she will attempt to perform the Incantation Demonata.

CF: But a mere child to dabble with such dark magic. Perhaps if you could reveal her to me. . . .

VM: You know I cannot speak her name until it is confirmed at trial, Regis. But do not worry, I will not allow her to complete the spell.

CF: But you must.

VM: Excuse me, Regis? I do not understand.

CF: It is a test, Venator. The Incantation *must* be performed. If she fails, you will take up the blade and draw your own blood.

VM: The Committee knows of this? The Conclave approves?

CF: Do not worry about the Conclave. This is my business. The Venators are loyal to me, are they not?

VM: But Regis—the Incantation. Are you sure?

CF: I am. When the time comes, do it. On my order.

SEVENTEEN

When Bliss was growing up, her family lived in one of those mega-mansions that were ubiquitous in River Oaks, a wealthy Houston suburb. Their house was the epitome of "Texas Excess," at twenty-eight thousand square feet. Bliss used to joke that it should have its own zip code. She had never felt comfortable in it, and preferred her grandparents' rambling ranch in the wilds of West Texas instead.

Despite their Yankee roots, her family was considered Lone Star aristocracy—their money made in oil, cattle, and well . . . mostly oil. The story the Llewellyns liked to tell was how the family patriarch had scandalized his upper-crust family by dropping out of Yale to work at an oil field. He'd quickly learned the ropes, buying up thousands of acres of oil-rich land to become the luckiest oil baron in the entire state. Was it luck or due to vampire ability, Bliss wondered now.

Forsyth was the youngest son of the youngest son. Her grandfather was a rebel who'd stayed East after boarding school, married his Andover sweetheart, a Connecticut debutante, and raised their son in her family's Fifth Avenue apartment, until bad luck on the stock market sent the family back to the Texas homestead.

Her grandfather had been one of her favorite people. He'd retained his Texan drawl even after his years in the Northeast, and he'd had an ironic, saucy sense of humor. He liked to say he didn't belong anywhere and therefore belonged everywhere. He was nostalgic about his life in New York, but he'd dug in and took over the family business when no one else wanted the ranch, preferring to move to the glass metropolises of Dallas or San Antonio instead. She wished Pap-Pap had stuck around; what was the point of being a vampire if you had to live a human-length lifetime anyway, and then had to wait to get called up again for the next cycle?

Bliss had grown up among many cousins, and until she moved to New York and turned fifteen, had always assumed there was nothing particularly special or interesting about her. Perhaps it was a willful ignorance. There had been signs, she realized later on: her older cousins hinting of "the change," furtive giggles from the already initiated, her father's rotating secretaries who, she now understood, served as his human familiars. It just recently occurred to Bliss how odd it was that no one ever spoke of her real mother.

BobiAnne was the only mother she'd ever known. Bliss

had an uneasy relationship with her tacky, over-protective stepmother, who showered Bliss with affection while ignoring her own child, Bliss's half sister, Jordan. BobiAnne, with her furs and diamonds and ridiculous decorating schemes, had tried too hard to replace the mother Bliss had never known, and Bliss couldn't hate her for it. On the other hand, she couldn't love her for it either.

Forsyth had married BobiAnne while Bliss was still in the cradle, and Jordan had been born four years later. A silent and strange child, who was pudgy to Bliss's willowy form, pasty to Bliss's ivory complexion, and difficult in comparison to Bliss's easygoing temperament. Yet Bliss couldn't imagine life without her younger sister, and displayed a fierce protectiveness whenever BobiAnne would tease or insult her own progeny. For her part, Jordan adored her sister when she wasn't mocking her. It was a normal sibling relationship—full of spats and bickering, and yet bolstered by a faithful and abiding loyalty.

One always took the most important things in life for granted, Bliss thought, when a few days after the fashion show she took a taxi to the uppermost reaches of Manhattan. She directed the driver to the Columbia-Presbyterian hospital.

"Are you family?" inquired the guard at the reception desk, pushing forward a visitor sheet for her to sign.

Bliss hesitated. She touched the photograph hidden in her coat pocket for luck. It was similar to one her father kept in his wallet, a copy of which she'd found in a jewelry case and now held in her hands.

"Yes."

"Top floor. Last room at the end of the hallway."

She wished she had someone to accompany her, but she couldn't think of anyone she could ask. Schuyler would certainly demand an explanation, and Bliss would not be able to provide a reasonable one. "Um, I think you and I might be sisters?" just sounded too preposterous.

As for Dylan, Bliss had shoved all thoughts of him to the back of her mind. She knew she should check up on him, especially now that he'd stopped trying to contact her, but she was too angry and humiliated to return to that awful room at the Chelsea Hotel. The strange tics she'd observed: the guttural speech, the high laugh, the strange babble of languages only made her more fearful of him. Bliss knew it was wishful thinking, but she couldn't help hoping that maybe things would just go back to normal. She'd promised Schuyler and Oliver she would deal with it—turn him in to the Committee and the Conclave—but so far she kept finding excuses not to. Even if she'd decided not to be attracted to him anymore, she couldn't find it in her heart to rat on him either.

She had other things to worry about, even though she knew she wasn't going to find any answers at the hospital. Allegra was in a coma, after all. And it was useless to try bringing up the subject with her father.

All her life, Bliss had been told that her mother had died when she was young. That "Charlotte Potter" had been a schoolteacher her father had met during his first political campaign, when he'd run for state congressman. Now Bliss wondered if Charlotte Potter had ever existed. Certainly there were no wedding albums, no trinkets, no heirlooms to indicate any such woman had ever been married to her father. For the longest time she had assumed it was because BobiAnne did not want reminders of the former Mrs. Llewellyn.

She didn't know anything about her real mother's family, and with her acute vampire memory, could go back to the time when she'd first asked her father what her real mother's name was. She was five years old, and her father had just read her a bedtime story. "Charlotte Potter," he'd told her cheerfully. "Your mother's name was Charlotte Potter."

Bliss had been charmed. "Just like *Charlotte's Web*!" she'd squealed. And her last name was just like the woman who wrote all those books on her shelves, Beatrix Potter.

More and more, Bliss suspected that her father had just made it up. The other day when she'd mentioned the name to Forsyth, he had simply looked blank.

Bliss walked to the end of the hall and found the room. She pushed the door open and slipped inside.

Allegra Van Alen's room was as cold as a meat locker. The woman slumbering in the bed did not move. Bliss approached the bedside tentatively, feeling like an intruder. Allegra looked peaceful, ageless, her face unlined. She was like a princess in a glass coffin: beautiful and still.

She thought that when she finally saw Allegra she would sense something—know for sure whether she was related to her or not. But there was nothing. Bliss touched the necklace hidden underneath her shirt for comfort, then reached over to hold Allegra's hand, feeling her papery skin. She closed her eyes and tried to access her past lives, her memories, to see if she had any knowledge of Gabrielle.

In flashes she would catch a glimpse of someone who looked familiar, who might have been her, but Bliss wasn't sure. In the end, the woman in the bed was as much a stranger as the nurse in the hallway.

"Allegra?" Bliss whispered. It seemed presumptuous to call her "mother." "It's me. I'm . . . Bliss. I don't know if you remember me, but I think you might be my . . ." Bliss suddenly stopped short. She felt a pain in her chest, as if she couldn't breathe. What was she doing here? She had to go. She had to leave immediately.

She was right; she would find no answers here. She would never know the truth. Her father would never tell her, and Allegra *could* not.

Bliss left, troubled and confused, still seeking answers to questions she kept in her heart.

She did not know that when she left the room, Allegra Van Alen began to scream.

ommittee meetings never started on time, so Mimi didn't worry when her conference call with her bonding planner ran a little longer than she'd planned. Ever since Lawrence had been installed as Regis, the meetings had less and less to do with social planning and fund-raising and more to do with, in her opinion, totally redundant vampire lessons.

Edmund Oelrich, the doddering senile goat from the Conclave who was the new chief warden, didn't run as tight a ship as the late Priscilla Dupont, and was completely ignorant of the fact that if they wanted to secure the right honorary chairs for the annual spring gala for the ballet in May, they should have sent feelers out a few weeks ago. As it was, all the former First Ladies were already unavailable, and the governor's wife was immersed in her husband's latest scandal. At this rate they would have to settle for the mayor's girlfriend, who wasn't remotely fashionable or at all interested in doing social work under the guise of social-climbing.

Mimi entered the library room at Duchesne, found a seat in the back, and tapped on the Bluetooth device attached to her ear as an excuse for not greeting her friends. She thought the Committee's lessons were a complete waste of time. She'd been adept at all her skills since transformation, and it galled her that other vampires were so slow. Today they were supposed to learn more about *mutatio*, the ability to change into the elements: fire, water, air. Mimi sighed. She had been disappearing into a fog since she was eleven. She had "developed" early, as they say.

"Sorry, could you repeat that again?" she asked, shaking the tiny silver receiver wedged in her ear. "You think we could have it at the White House? No?"

The firm she'd hired, Elizabeth Tilton Events, had recently orchestrated a five-day extravaganza in Cartagena, wherein Don Alejandro Castañeda, the Blue Blood heir to his father's sugar-and-beverage fortune, had been bonded to his vampire twin, Danielle Russell, a recent Brown graduate. Mimi and Jack had represented the family, and Mimi had been a little miffed when the talk at the rehearsal dinner was about how extraordinary everything had been. The best man had announced that "the next bonding will have to be on the moon, since no one else is going to top this!"

Mimi was sure going to try.

"Darling," Lizbet Tilton cooed. "I'm sorry, but with the new administration, the Rose Garden is out of the question. I don't think we contributed enough to the campaign. But there has to be somewhere else you'd like to have it."

"What about Buckingham, then? I'm sure my father can call in a favor."

Lizbet laughed heartily. "Sweetheart, what century are you in? Have you got your lifetimes confused? Even though you're a Royal, that branch of the clan has never forgiven us for leaving. Besides, they're terribly strict these days. Even Charles and Camilla had to get married off-site."

Mimi pouted. "Well, I guess we could do it in on the island," she said, noticing that Schuyler and Bliss had just entered the room. Mimi sent a quick suggestion and caused Schuyler to suddenly trip. Ha. Someone sure wasn't doing their *occludo* lessons. Schuyler's mind was as open as a wound.

"You mean your dad's place in Sandy Cay?" Lizbet asked. "That would be fabulous." The Forces owned their own private island in the Bahamas. "Everyone could jet down for the weekend, and if they don't have wings we could charter a plane. We just did that for Alex and Dani in Colombia."

Mimi *so* did not want her bonding to be just like anyone else's.

"What about Italy?" Lizbet suggested. "One of the ancestral palaces? You guys still have that place in Tuscany?"

"Um, no. Not Italy. Bad memories?" Mimi chided, glaring at the group that was staring at her. The chief warden and the rest of the senior committee had finally arrived, and lessons were about to commence.

"Right. Sorry."

"You know," Lizbet said thoughtfully, "with all the hoopla of everyone getting bonded everywhere, no one has done a five-star New York bonding in decades."

"Here? Just at home?" Mimi frowned. That did not sound special at all.

Up front, Edmund Oelrich was shuffling papers at the podium and greeting the well-preserved women who made up the senior committee.

"Saint John the Divine is a fabulous Gothic cathedral. You could wear a train longer than Princess Di's. And we could get the Boys Choir of Harlem. It would be properly angelic."

Mimi considered the suggestion. It was indeed a beautiful church, she told Lizbet, and they could have the reception at the Temple of Dendur at the Metropolitan Museum afterward. Charles was a museum trustee and had been particularly generous that year. She waved to Jack, who had just come in the door. Her brother joined her and gave a quick smile.

"Who are you talking to?" he mouthed.

"So, we're on the same page here? Saint John's? And then the Met?" Lizbet was asking. "And you did say you wanted to invite the whole Four Hundred, yes?"

"Done and done!" Mimi said with satisfaction. She put away her phone and smiled at her brother. Now that she knew his secret, she noticed that he looked everywhere in the room except toward the corner where Schuyler was sitting.

Schuyler's sidekick, that equally annoying human Oliver, arrived soon after. That was another travesty—letting humans into their exclusive meetings. Charles would never have allowed it during his tenure. But Lawrence had made it clear he expected the Conduits to undergo their own training as well, and what better way to learn about their calling than to join the Committee.

Mimi sensed Jack tense by her side. Oliver had kissed Schuyler on the cheek. That was interesting. She used her vampire sense to zero in on Oliver's neck. She spotted the telltale bite marks immediately. They were undetectable to the human eye, but glaring to the vampire sight. So. The little half-blood had made her best friend her familiar.

Well.

It gave Mimi an idea. If Schuyler wasn't going to give up her pathetic little liaison with Jack, then maybe she could be forced to.

Oliver could prove useful.

Mimi would have to act fast. She'd told Lizbet she wanted her bonding to take place in three months.

NINETEEN

Unlike Mimi, Bliss enjoyed the Committee's new agenda. She liked discovering and using her vampire abilities, instead of merely memorizing boring facts about their history, or stuffing envelopes and critiquing caterers for extravagant events that she didn't look forward to attending. Lessons got her blood pumping. She was thrilled to find herself adept at some of the more difficult tasks, like the *mutatio*, for instance.

The senior committee had asked the younger members to arrange themselves into groups of two or three while they practiced the delicate art of metamorphosis.

"All vampires should be able to change into smoke, or air, or fog; although most of us can transform into fire and water as well. As you might be aware, The Conspiracy saw to it that the false legends about our people perpetuated in Red Blood history are based on a modicum of truth." Dorothea

Rockefeller, their guest lecturer, chuckled as she said this. The Conspiracy was a great source of amusement to the Committee.

"They also thought it might be suitable if the humans were led to believe that our kind can only transform into bats or rats or other creatures of the night. That way the Red Bloods would be lulled into a false sense of security during daylight hours. And while it is true that those of us who have the ability to shape-shift may choose these rather repulsive physical shapes, most of us do not. In fact, our lady Gabrielle chose a dove as her *mutatus*. If you are one of the few who can transform at will, you will find a shape that suits your abilities. Do not be surprised when it is one that you did not expect."

Bliss was one of the lucky few. She found she could switch from girl to smoke and back again, and then tried out other forms—a white horse, a black crow, a spider monkey— before settling into the shape of a golden lioness.

But Schuyler simply stood in the middle of the room, getting more and more frustrated with each failed attempt. "Maybe it's because I'm half human," she sighed when yet another try at forcing her matter to change into a different configuration resulted in her simply falling onto the floor, still herself.

"Hey, what's wrong with being human?" Oliver asked, watching with fascination as Mimi Force transformed herself into a phoenix, a column of fire, and a red serpent in the space of three seconds. "Wow—she's good."

"Show-off," Bliss hissed. "Don't worry about her. And stop laughing, Ollie. You're distracting Schuyler!" Bliss tried not to be too smug about her success, but it was satisfying to know that Schuyler wasn't great at everything.

"Look, here's what you do. You're supposed to visualize your goal. You have to *be* the fog. Think like fog. Let your mind go blank. Can you feel it—a wispiness—it starts in the edge of your skin, and then . . ."

Schuyler obediently closed her eyes. "Okay, I'm thinking fog. Golden Gate. San Francisco. Little cat feet. I don't know . . . it's not happening."

"Sshhhh," Bliss admonished. She could already feel the transformation begin, could feel all her senses shift, could feel her very being disappear into a soft gray cloud. She was having fun imagining how she could use this new talent, when she had another vision. It hit her with a bang. The starkness of the image was like a punch in the gut.

Dylan.

If he'd looked merely disheveled before, he was worse now. His clothing was in tatters, his shirt ripped to shreds, his jeans torn, and his hair wild. He looked like he hadn't eaten or slept in weeks. He was standing in front of the school gates, shaking the bars and raving like a madman.

"What's wrong?" Schuyler asked immediately when Bliss stumbled.

"Dylan. He's here."

That was all she needed to say.

The three of them ran out of the Committee meeting, ignoring the curious faces of the other members, leaving the library, and running down the stairs. Their vampire speed meant Schuyler and Bliss arrived at the gates ahead of Oliver, who was gasping as he tried to keep up with them.

Duchesne was located on a quiet corner of Ninety-sixth Street, on Prep School Row. Since it was mid-afternoon, the streets were practically deserted, save for a nanny or two pushing a stroller toward the park.

The boy who stood in the middle of the sidewalk violently shaking the gates looked like a prophet from a bygone age, a throwback to a time of preachers and pontificators, when ragged men warned about the End Of The World. There was almost no sign of the teenage boy who had wanted to grow up to play guitar like Jimi Hendrix and had been the instigator of countless pranks.

"ABOMINATION!" he thundered when he saw them.

"It's my fault," Bliss cried, already close to tears at the sight of Dylan. "I know I promised I was going to tell the Conclave about him, but I couldn't. And I didn't check up on him . . . I left him and I ignored him . . . I wanted him to just go away. It's all my fault."

"No, it's mine," Schuyler said. "I was going to tell Lawrence, but—"

"It's all our fault," Oliver said firmly. "We should have done something about him, but we didn't. Look, we've got to get him out of here. People are going to start asking questions," he said as an elderly woman walking a poodle crossed the street and shot a puzzled look in their direction. "We don't want the police involved."

Dylan suddenly lunged toward them, clawing through the bars and gargling in a language they didn't understand.

Schuyler just barely ducked his reach. "We've got to get to him before he uses the glom on us again."

Bliss immediately transformed into the golden lioness. She was a sight to behold—a stalking, ruthless creature. She leaped over the gate and padded up to Dylan, who raged at her. *"Devil spawn! TRAITOR!"* he hissed.

Bliss cornered him against the iron bars and bared her teeth. She reared back on her hind legs and shoved him with her giant golden paws. Dylan cringed and whimpered, cowering with his hands over his head.

"She's got him!" Oliver yelled, motioning to Schuyler to move toward Bliss's right flank.

Schuyler ran to Bliss's side. She looked Dylan in the eyes. Saw the rage, anger, and confusion there. She wavered. This was no monster. This was a wounded animal.

But Oliver had no qualms. "SCHUYLER! DO IT! NOW!"

"Dormi!" she ordered, and waved her hand in front of Dylan's face.

Dylan slumped and fell to the ground. Bliss turned back into herself and knelt by his side.

"He'll sleep until he is commanded to wake up," Schuyler told them.

Oliver knelt beside Bliss, and they were able to make a makeshift straitjacket from Dylan's sweater. The lines on his face slowly smoothed away. Asleep, he looked docile and peaceful.

"We've got to turn him over to the Committee; this has gone on long enough," Oliver said. "I know you don't want to, Bliss, but it's best for him. Maybe they can help him."

"They don't *help* Silver Bloods—they destroy them. You know that," Bliss said bitterly.

"But maybe . . ."

"I'll take him to my father," Bliss decided. "I might be able to plead his case with Forsyth. Get him to show Dylan some mercy because he's my friend. He'll know what to do."

Schuyler nodded. Forsyth should be able to deal with Dylan. Meanwhile, the Llewellyns' Rolls-Royce pulled up to the curb. They bundled Dylan into the backseat and strapped him in next to Bliss.

"He'll be okay," Schuyler assured.

"Yeah," Bliss said, even though she knew that none of them believed it anymore. The car pulled away, and she raised her hand in good-bye. Oliver returned the wave, while Schuyler simply looked stricken. Finally the car turned the corner and she couldn't see them anymore.

When Bliss arrived at Penthouse des Reves, her family's extravagant triplex apartment on the top of one of the most exclusive buildings on Park Avenue, BobiAnne was consulting with her astrologer in the "casual" sitting room. Bliss's stepmother was a big-haired Texan socialite who was dripping in diamonds even in the early afternoon. Bliss's half sister, Jordan, was doing homework on a nearby coffee table. The two of them looked up in surprise at Bliss's entry.

"What on earth?" BobiAnne cried, leaping from her chair at the sight of her stepdaughter and the bound, unconscious boy.

"It's Dylan," Bliss said, as if that would explain everything. She was frightfully calm as she addressed her family. She had no idea how they would react at the sight of him, especially since he was so dirty. BobiAnne had a heart palpitation when someone forgot to use a coaster or left sweaty handprints on the Japanese wallpaper.

"The boy who disappeared," Jordan whispered, her eyes round and frightened.

"Yes. There's something wrong with him. He's . . . not quite all there. I have to tell Dad." Bliss confessed to everything—Dylan's unexpected return, how she'd hid him in the Chelsea Hotel—and gave them the Cliff's Notes version of his previous attacks. "But we're all fine," she assured. "Don't worry about me. Help *him*," she said, gently setting Dylan down on the nearest chaise longue.

"You did the right thing," BobiAnne said, pressing Bliss to her chest and smothering her with her perfume. "He'll be safe here with us."

pring in New York was a mirage. The city turned from brutal winter to brutal summer with barely a gap in between. After the winter snows melted, there would be a few days of rain, and then the sun would shine mercilessly, turning the city into one big sauna. Like her fellow residents, Schuyler prized what little spring they had. As she walked across Ninety-sixth Street with Bliss after school, she smiled when she noticed the first fragile buds of the season. However much her life had changed, she could still count on the tulips to blossom in Central Park.

She picked off a tiny yellow flower from a nearby bush and tucked it in her hair. Duchesne was starting to unwind in its last few months before summer vacation. The seniors had all received their college acceptances, and teachers held half their classes in the outdoor courtyards.

Bliss told her that Dylan was being taken care of—and

not in a bad way. Forsyth had been more than sympathetic to Dylan's situation. The senator had told her there might still be hope for him, even if he had been corrupted, since it took a long time for a Blue Blood to turn into a Silver Blood. There might still be time to halt the process. Forsyth had put him in a place where he could be observed and rehabilitated.

"Basically, he's in rehab," Bliss explained as they walked past the familiar landmarks of the neighborhood, dodging a group of scowling Nightingale-Bamford girls in their blue-and-white uniforms. "You know how Charlie Bank and Honor Leslie had to go to Transitions last year? And everyone thought it was because of drugs?" Bliss asked, naming two Duchesne students who had disappeared from school for months at a time.

"Uh-huh." Schuyler nodded.

"Well, they weren't druggies. Their transformations were freaking them out. They were having delusions, they couldn't separate the past from the present. They were attacking humans, violating the Code. So they were sent away to deal with it. Rehab's a good cover, don't you think? The humans think they're there to dry out, which I guess is true in a way."

It always amazed Schuyler how the vampires found a way to disguise their real lives by integrating into regular human society, but Bliss explained it was actually the other way around. "Apparently, the Mayo Clinic, Hazelden, and all those famous rehab centers were founded by Blue Bloods. They had to start catering to human problems when it became fashionable to go. You think he'll be okay?" Bliss asked.

Schuyler didn't want to give Bliss any false hope, but she thought it would be cruel to say otherwise. "I'm sure they'll try their best."

Bliss sighed. "Yeah."

They made plans to go visit Dylan in a few days, and Schuyler said good-bye at Eighty-sixth to catch the Fifth Avenue bus.

All week she had forced thoughts of Mimi's warning from her mind. Was Mimi telling the truth? Was she putting Jack in danger? She had wanted to ask Lawrence about it, but she had been too ashamed. What had her grandfather told her? *You must have noticed he is drawn to you. Thank goodness you are not drawn to him. It would spell disaster to both of you.*

How could she tell her grandfather that he was wrong. That she did return Jack Force's affections. That she was weak and pathetic when Lawrence believed she was so strong. She could not. She told herself she couldn't bother him with such a silly thing as her love life anyway, while he was out there dealing with a problem as grave and serious as the possible destruction of the very essence of the Blue Bloods' existence. She was starting to worry about Lawrence. There hadn't been a message from him in days.

Her grandfather had been wary of using the normal means of communication, and once he'd arrived in Rio had relied exclusively on telepathy to get in touch and let her know everything was okay. So far he'd only complained about the weather (steamy) and the food (too spicy). He hadn't addressed the problem of Corcovado, and Schuyler didn't know if that was good or bad.

There had been no opportunity to ask Jack about his sister's dire predictions either. They had been unable to meet since the night of Dylan's attack. Mimi, Schuyler knew, was taking up all of his free time.

When she arrived at the town house, Jack was in the living room, speaking to his father. Charles was in his bathrobe. The former leader of the Blue Bloods now spent his days in his study. He didn't even look as if he had showered that day. Schuyler felt pity and annoyance. He had caused her so much heartache. She'd had to avoid everyone she loved because of him. She'd believed his threats, but lately it looked as though Charles was only a threat to himself. But then she realized if Charles had not dragged her to his home, maybe she and Jack would never have had the chance to find out just how much they truly liked each other.

"Hey." Jack smiled. "You're back early."

"I made the bus this time," she said, setting her school things down on a nearby table. She still didn't feel comfortable in their house, but on the other hand, she was tired of tiptoeing around the place as if she didn't belong there.

"Hello, Schuyler," Charles grunted.

"Charles," she said coldly.

The former Regis tightened the belt on his robe and shuffled off to his den, leaving the two of them alone.

"Is she here?" Schuyler asked, looking around the opulent space that was the Forces' living room. Decorated in lush, French-Victorian style, the room was closely packed with rare antiques, jaw-droppingly familiar museum-quality art, and sumptuous fabrics. Her senses told her that Mimi was not around the premises. But who knew.

"No. She's at some sort of tasting," he replied.

Schuyler sat next to him on a gilded velvet "kissing chair" dating to the sixteenth-century and so named because a couple had to sit side-by-side and facing each other. "Jack." She looked at his face. The face she loved so much. "I want to ask you something."

"Shoot," Jack said, stretching his legs out in front of him and loping his long arm over the edge of the chair so that his fingers rested lightly on her shoulders. She tingled at his slightest touch.

"Is it true that the bond between you and—"

"I don't want to talk about the bond," Jack said, cutting her off and withdrawing his arm. His face turned cold, and for a moment she saw a flash of his true nature, saw the dark angel that he was. The angel who had wrought destruction in Paradise, the one who would sound the trumpet to the Apocalypse when it came. His was the face of Abbadon, the enforcer, the hammer blow, the most dangerous soldier in the army of the Almighty.

"But I want to know—"

"Shh." Jack turned to her and pressed a hand on her cheek. "Let's not . . ."

"But Mimi . . ." Just as Schuyler said her name, she sensed a presence at the front doorway. Mimi was home, or just about to be. Quicker than a blink, or at maximum vampire speed, Schuyler left the living room and ran to her bedroom, shutting the door behind her.

When Mimi entered mere seconds later, carrying several shopping bags with her, she found Jack reading a book by himself.

Schuyler and Jack weren't alone again that evening. The entire family gathered for their mandatory dinner a few hours later. Once a week, Trinity Burden, their mother, required that the children be home to join their parents for dinner. Schuyler had once dreamed of a nuclear family, of a life that included a loving mother, an attentive father, and siblings who would tease each other over the meat and potatoes.

Of course, the Forces were nothing like this.

Meals at home were served in the formal dining room, on a table so large and intimidating, each person was seated a good two feet away from the other. Each entrée was served by a butler on a silver tray, and the menu never varied—it was always French, it was always rich and complicated, and it was always perfectly delicious. Yet Schuyler missed Hattie's no-nonsense slapdash cooking, and longed for simple, unpretentious servings of macaroni-and-cheese or a pot roast that didn't require a red-wine reduction and an accent to pronounce.

Conversation was stale or nonexistent. Charles continued to be lost in his own world, while Trinity tried to engage the twins in perfunctory chatter about their lives. Jack was courteous while Mimi was simply curt. At least someone other than Schuyler thought these dinners were a farce and a waste of time.

"So, Jack and I have an announcement," Mimi said, when the dessert course arrived, a flaming peaches jubilee. "We've decided on the date of our bonding."

Schuyler tried to compose her face but found she could not help staring at Jack, who looked as impassive as ever. Their bonding! So soon . . .

Mimi reached out to hold her brother's hand in hers.

"It's a little early, don't you think?" Trinity asked, looking concerned. "You have a lot of time."

Yes, Schuyler thought. Lots and lots of time. Possibly forever.

Charles coughed. "Remember that age is an illusion among us, Trinity. You are starting to think like a Red Blood. The sooner they bond, the stronger they will be. A toast is in order. To the twins."

"To us!" Mimi crowed, clinking her glass against Jack's. The crystal rang like a deep booming bell.

"To the twins," Schuyler whispered. She sipped but found she could not swallow the wine in her glass.

Later that night as Schuyler dreamed, she received a message from Lawrence. The sending was easier in the dream state, he explained. It was not as shocking to the senses, and asleep her mind held no distractions.

"Corcovado secure. All is well."

iring Lizbet Tilton was the best decision she could have made, Mimi thought, congratulating herself on her savvy. Lizbet ran a very tight ship, and in short order the venues were locked in on the requested dates, contracts drafted, budgets balanced, deposits made. Earlier that afternoon Trinity and Mimi had gone over color schemes and menus with the caterer and the interior designer. Everything was operating like clockwork; although you'd think it was the doomsday clock, the way Jack was acting.

"Do you know what this is about?" he asked, meeting Mimi in Trinity's sitting room the next evening.

Their "mother"—Mimi always thought of the word in air quotes, since Trinity was as much her mother as Jack was her brother—had requested their presence before dinner. She had intimated that she wanted to talk to them about something important concerning their bonding.

"I have a feeling." Mimi smiled. She ruffled Jack's hair, and in return he put a hand on her waist and drew her close to him. They had always been affectionate, and even though she was aware of his continuing duplicity, she could not harden her heart against him. Jack hadn't agreed to bonding so early in the cycle, but on the other hand, he hadn't done anything to stop it either.

Perhaps the dalliance with Schuyler was simply that. Jack was just using her as an amusement. A side dish. Mimi certainly understood. She had found a tasty new familiar, and had been so voracious in her appetite she had almost killed the boy the other day. He would be all right; nothing that rest and a week away from a certain blond vampire couldn't cure.

Mimi looked around with approval. Trinity's home office was famous among her set for being the most lavish and impeccable. Hung on the velvet walls were life-size portraits of seventeenth- and eighteenth-century aristocrats by Vigée-LeBrun and Winterhalter. There was an Erard piano in the corner—the very same one Chopin used to compose his études. The *bonheurs du jour*, a small, elegant writing table where Trinity wrote her one-word thank you cards ("Bravo!" was her usual exhortation after attending a friend's dinner party) was originally commissioned for the Grand Trianon.

Mimi decided that when she came into her massive inheritance, and she and Jack bought their own place at 740 Park, she would hire the same decorator.

A few minutes later, Trinity entered the room holding

two long ebony boxes embossed with gold filigree. Mimi's senses shifted, her memories racing, and she suddenly knew why they were there. "But where's Charles?" she cried. "We can't do this without him, can we?"

"I tried, my dear. But he won't leave his study. He's just . . ." Trinity shook her shoulders ever so slightly. Mimi understood that her mother adhered to a rigid code of etiquette. As distressed as she might be about her husband's condition, she would never admit to it or show any outward display of exasperation. She was a woman who was fundamentally unequipped to make a scene.

Charles's deterioration since losing his position as Regis of the Coven was something that the Forces never spoke about. It baffled and troubled them, but there was nothing they could do about it. They assumed Charles would simply snap out of it one day. Meanwhile, the company and all its holdings was run by a highly efficient board of directors, who had stopped inquiring as to whether their chairman and founder would ever attend another meeting.

"It's all right," Jack assured his twin. He too knew what was about to happen and couldn't disguise the excitement in his voice. "We don't need him."

"Are you sure?" Mimi asked, looking disappointed. "But without the Archangel's blessing . . ."

"They will be just as deadly," Jack soothed. "Nothing can change their power. Their power comes from the two of us." He nodded to Trinity. "Shall we begin, Mother?"

In answer, Trinity bowed her head. "I shall be honored to perform the rite." She closed the door quietly and dimmed the overhead lights. The boxes on the coffee table emanated a soft, hazy glow.

"I regret my hastiness in judging the precipitancy of your bonding. I was wrong, forgive me. It is perhaps only that I am saddened that I myself can no longer be bonded to my twin."

Mimi knew Trinity's story. Trinity was Sandalphon, the Angel of Silence. She had lost her twin to the Silver Bloods during the battle in Rome. Trinity had married Charles only in the Red Blood sense when his twin, Allegra, had broken their bond. It was a marriage of convenience, nothing more. Trinity mourned the angel Salgiel's passing still.

Trinity opened the cases. Nestled inside were two swords holstered in jeweled scabbards. Swords that would be worn underneath their garments at the bonding. Swords that they would now be allowed to use in the fight against the Croatan.

She picked up the first sword still in its scabbard and turned to Jack. "Kneel, Abbadon."

Jack stood up from his chair and walked to stand in front of Trinity. He knelt before her, his head bowed low.

Trinity raised the sword above her head. "With the authority of the Heavens vested in me, I, Sandalphon, confer upon you all the rights and privileges appertaining thereto as the true owner of *Eversor Orbis*."

World-Breaker.

She then tapped Jack's right and left shoulder with the sword. "Rise, Abbadon of the Dark."

Jack rose with a grim smile on his face as he accepted his sword. Trinity smiled proudly. Then she turned to Mimi.

"Kneel, Azrael."

Mimi took a moment to get in position, due to her high heels. Trinity picked up the second sword and once again raised it over her head.

"With the authority of the Heavens vested in me, I, Sandalphon, confer upon you all the rights and privileges appertaining thereto as the true owner of *Eversor Lumen*."

Light-Destroyer.

Mimi felt the sword tap her lightly on both shoulders. Then she stood up with a broad smile on her face. She turned to Jack, who nodded. Together the twins unsheathed their swords and lifted them aloft, pointing them to the Heavens.

"We accept these weapons as our divine right. Forged in Heaven, cast on Earth, they are our attendants in our search for Redemption."

Trinity joined them as they finished the litany of the Swords.

"Use them only in direst need.

"Keep them hidden from foes.

"Strike only to kill."

While they had received their swords at every bonding over the centuries, they had not been truly unsheathed in millennia. The Silver Bloods had been vanquished, or so they had believed. Mimi looked with wonder at the shining weapon in her hand. She remembered its weight and the sharpness of its blade. Remembered the terror it had once wrought in her enemies.

She noticed how Abbadon was holding his delicately, lovingly. One's sword was an extension of one's self. Unique, irreplaceable, unforgettable. Vampire swords changed shape and color and size. When needed they could become as wide as axes or as narrow as needles.

At the bonding, she would wear it on her hip, under the silk petticoats that would give her dress its shape.

Trinity turned the lights back to their full brightness. "All right, then." She nodded as if they had just finished talking about something small and trivial instead of having completed something wondrous and life-changing. In the afternoon light, with the sound of taxicabs zooming down the avenues and the metallic beeps from Trinity's fax machine (receiving yet another copy of a press clip in which she had been written up), it was hard to imagine the world as full of primitive, hidden dangers. How to reconcile a world with instant-messaging and twenty-four-hour news channels with the world of steel and blood.

But that is what their people did: they evolved, they adapted, they survived.

"Pretty cool, huh?" Jack asked, as they took leave of their mother and went their separate ways.

"You betcha." Mimi nodded, tucking the ebony case under her arm. She ran up to her room and shoved it in the back of her closet behind a rack of shoes.

She was late for Pilates. If she was going to be the most beautiful bride the Coven had ever seen, she'd better haul ass to her trainer's studio right away. She had arms to sculpt.

May 9, 1993

Dear Forsyth,

As you know, I have deeply appreciated your steadfast loyalty and friendship to the Van Alen family. It troubles me that we have been estranged of late due to your decision to run and hold a Red Blood office in direct violation of The Code. While I am not convinced you made the right choice, I respect it.

I am writing to beseech you to change your mind concerning your decision not to bring the new spirit of the watcher into your family.

I must insist that you reconsider. We need vigilance more than ever, and the wisdom of the Watcher to guide us on our way. I fear Charles and his arrogance will bring nothing but doom to our people.

Forsyth, I appeal to you in friendship: Take the spirit of the Watcher into your family. As a safeguard against the forces of the Dark.

Your friend,
Cordelia Van Alen

ransitions Residential Treatment Center was located in a sprawling multi-building campus in upstate New York. Oliver had offered to drive Bliss and Schuyler, since he had recently gotten his license along with a hot new Mercedes G500. The boxy custom-made silver SUV was his latest source of pride.

Schuyler was glad to get away. She'd been feeling guilty about what had happened to Dylan, how much they'd failed him by neglecting to alert the Conclave about his condition as soon as possible. Hopefully the Elders would know the best course of action. Bliss told them her father assured her that Dylan would come to no harm at their hands and would be given the best treatment possible, but she wanted to see it with her own eyes—they all did.

In the backseat, Bliss fluctuated between being kind of bummed and being a little too cheerfully manic, Schuyler noticed. She'd been morose and silent when they left, probably worried about Dylan and what condition they would find him in, and Schuyler was glad when halfway through the trip out of the city Bliss perked up and began to jabber energetically over the GPS.

"Peanut M&M's?" Bliss offered, leaning over with a large open yellow bag.

"No thanks," Oliver said, keeping his eyes on the road.

"Sure," Schuyler agreed. It was funny how the Committee couldn't predict everything: even though they were vampires they hadn't lost their taste for candy.

It was pleasant to leave Duchesne, if only for a day. Everyone at school knew all the details of Mimi and Jack's upcoming bonding already (or at least the Blue Bloods did) and couldn't stop talking about it. The others just thought the Forces were throwing a fabulous party that they weren't invited to again, and in a way their assumption was correct. Schuyler was sick of hearing about Mimi's dress and how this bonding compared to all the past ones in their shared history. Piper Crandall constantly reminded everyone that she had been a bondsmaid for Mimi three times already.

It was depressing to think that Jack and Mimi had been together for such an incomprehensibly long time. She almost couldn't believe it and didn't want to think about it right then, and busied herself by playing with all the buttons on the shiny new dashboard computer. "Dude, this is like, the most luxurious army vehicle in the world. Check this out!

This is the button that launches the M-15s," she joked.

"Careful, that's the red button that destroys the world," Oliver said gamely, following the GPS's robotic instructions as he steered the car over the George Washington Bridge. Traffic was light on the highway.

It was the first time they'd cut school all semester. Duchesne students were allowed several cuts per year; the school was so progressive that even rebellion was written into the curriculum. Some kids, like Mimi Force, pushed this policy to its limits, but most didn't even take advantage of it. The school was filled with overachieving strivers who would sooner stay in class than blow a chance at getting into an Ivy. Every day counted.

"You guys know that this could ruin my GPA," Oliver complained as he looked over his shoulder to change lanes and get ahead of a Honda that was tooling around below the speed limit.

"Relax for once, will you?" Schuyler chided. "All the seniors have been cutting since they got their acceptance letters." Oliver could be such a stick-in-the-mud sometimes. Always following rules. He was a total nerd when it came to academics.

"Yeah, aren't you legacy at Harvard anyway?" Bliss asked.

"College seems like such a weird thing, doesn't it?" Schuyler mused.

"I know what you mean. Before we found out about the

Committee, I thought I might go to Vassar, you know? Major in Art History or something." Bliss said. "I kind of liked the idea of studying Northern Renaissance art, and then working in a museum or gallery."

"What do you mean 'kind of liked'?" Schuyler asked.

"Yeah, you don't think that's going to happen anymore?" Oliver asked, flipping through the radio stations. Amy Winehouse was singing about how she didn't want to go to rehab ("No! No! No! No!"). Schuyler met Oliver's eyes, and they smiled.

"You guys, that is so not funny. Turn it off or change it," Bliss admonished. "I don't know. I kind of don't think I'm going to college. Sometimes I feel like I don't have a future," she said, twisting her necklace.

"Oh shush," Schuyler said, turning around so she could talk directly to Bliss while Oliver found something more appropriate on the satellite radio. "Of course you're going to college. We all are."

"You really believe that?" Bliss asked, sounding hopeful.

"Totally."

Conversation dropped to a lull after a few minutes, and Bliss drifted off to sleep. In the front seat, Schuyler chose the music, Oliver letting her DJ this time. "You like this song?" he asked, when she settled on a station playing a Rufus Wainwright tune.

"Don't you?" she asked, feeling as if she'd been caught red-handed. It was the same song she and Jack always played. She thought she could get away with listening to it in the car. Oliver had a bit of an emo streak in him. She liked to tease him that his musical tastes ran toward music-to-off-yourself-by.

"You'd think I would, right? But I don't."

"Why not?"

Oliver shrugged, looking at her sideways. "It's like . . . too blubbery or something. Ech."

"What do you mean?" Schuyler asked. "Blubbery?"

He shrugged. "I don't know, I just feel like love isn't supposed to be so . . . angsty, you know? Like, if it works, it shouldn't be so tortured."

"Huh," Schuyler said, wondering if she should change the station. It seemed traitorous to play a song that reminded her of another boy. "You are so unromantic."

"Am not."

"But you've never even been in love."

"You know that's not true."

Schuyler was silent. In the past month they had performed the *Caerimonia* twice. She knew she should take other familiars—vampires were told to rotate their humans so as not to tax them—but she'd been able to go longer than she'd thought without a feeding. And she had resisted taking other humans, not quite sure that Oliver would approve.

But Schuyler didn't want to think about their relationship—friendship—whatever it was. After Oliver's passionate outburst at the Odeon, it hadn't come up again.

She wanted to diffuse the tension she was starting to feel in the car. "Bet you can't even name one romantic movie you like," she teased.

She felt smug when a few minutes went by and Oliver was still unable to name one romantic movie he could profess to enjoy.

"*The Empire Strikes Back*," Oliver finally declared, tapping his horn at a Prius that wandered over the line.

"*The Empire Strikes Back*? The Star Wars movie? That's not romantic!" Schuyler huffed, fiddling with the air-conditioner controls.

"Au contraire, my dear, it's very romantic. The last scene, you know, when they're about to put Han in that freezing cryogenic chamber or whatever? Remember?"

Schuyler mmm-hmmmed.

"And Leia leans over the ledge and says, 'I love you.'"

"That's *cheesy*, not romantic," Schuyler argued, although she did like that part.

"Let me explain. What's romantic is what Han says back. Remember what he says to her? After she says 'I love you'?"

Schuyler grinned. Maybe Oliver had a point. "Han says, 'I know.'"

"Exactly." Oliver tapped the wheel. "He doesn't have to say anything so trite as 'I love you.' Because that's already understood. And *that's* romantic."

For once, Schuyler had to admit he was right.

TWENTY-THREE

When Bliss woke up from her nap, Oliver and Schuyler were snapping at each other in the front seat. "What're you guys arguing about now?" she asked, rubbing her eyes.

"Nothing," they chorused.

Bliss accepted their reticence without question. Those two always kept secrets from her, even when they didn't mean to.

"Okay, I guess we can stop for lunch, then," Schuyler finally said. Ah, so that was what it was about. Those two fought about everything. It had gotten worse since Oliver had become Schuyler's familiar. They acted more like an old married couple than before. On the surface, at least, they pretended their friendship was exactly the same. Which was just fine with Bliss; she didn't know if she could really stand any Schuyler-Ollie PDA.

"I'm just saying we're not going to do Dylan any good by going hungry." Oliver shrugged.

They pulled into a rest area, joining weary travelers at the vending machines and the food court.

Oliver observed that one of the novelties of growing up as city kids was that they were all addicted to suburban fast-food chains. While none of them would ever even consider going to a McDonald's in Manhattan—those places were basically ad-hoc homeless shelters—once they were out of city limits, the rules changed, and no one cared to eat expensive panini sandwiches and precious organic green salads. Bring on the supersized meals.

"God, I feel sick," Bliss said, sipping the last of her milk shake.

"I think I'm going to throw up," Oliver declared, crumpling the wrapper of his greasy hamburger and wiping his hands with several napkins.

"It's always fun to eat this stuff. But afterward . . ." Schuyler agreed, even though she was still picking at the fries.

"Afterward you always feel like you're going to hurl. Or that your cholesterol count just skyrocketed," Bliss said, making a face.

It was quiet when they climbed back into the car and felt the soporific effects of their heavy meal. A half hour later, the GPS blared "EXIT ON THE RIGHT IN FIVE HUNDRED METERS," and Oliver followed the signs up the ramp and down the road to a parking lot.

They had arrived.

The rehabilitation center grounds were immaculate. It looked more like a five-star resort, where celebrities went to hide after a lost weekend, rather than a high-priced treatment facility for floundering vampires. They saw a group practicing tai chi on the lawn, several others performing yoga poses, and clusters of people sitting in the grass in a circle.

"Group therapy," Bliss whispered as they made their way to the front door of the main building. "I asked Honor what it was like here, and she said there's a lot of past-lives-regression therapy."

They were greeted at the entrance by a slim, tanned woman in a white T-shirt and white pants. The effect was less clinical and more fashionable—like a New Age ashram.

"Can I help you?" the woman asked in a friendly manner.

"We're here to visit a friend," Bliss said, who had become the de facto spokesman for the trio.

"Name?"

"Dylan Ward."

The counselor checked the computer and nodded. "Do you have permission from the senator to visit this patient?"

"I'm, uh, his daughter," Bliss said, showing the woman her ID.

"Great. He's in the north campus, in a private cottage. Follow the path out the door, you'll see signs." She handed them visitor stickers. "Visiting hours are until four. The café is in the main building. It's International Day—I think it's Vietnamese. You guys like pho?"

"We already ate," Oliver said, and Bliss thought she sensed a hint of a smile in Oliver's words. "But thanks."

"It seems nice here," Schuyler said as they walked through the greenery.

"The Committee does do a good job, I'll give them that. Nothing but the best for the vamps." Oliver nodded and put on a pair of dark sunglasses.

Bliss couldn't believe how calm and organized everything was. This was where they put troubled Blue Bloods? Maybe she'd made a mistake in hiding Dylan for so long. Maybe they really could help him here. She began to feel less strained and more optimistic. Several patients waved to them as they passed.

Dylan's room was one of the nicer cottages, with a white picket fence and rosebushes growing by the windows. A nurse was sitting in an anteroom.

"He's sleeping. But let me see if he'll take visitors," she told them. She disappeared into the main room, and they could hear her talking in a soft, gentle voice to Dylan.

"He's ready for you." The nurse smiled and indicated that they were welcome to go inside.

Bliss exhaled and didn't realize she was holding her breath all this time. Dylan certainly looked better. He was sitting up in bed, there was color in his cheeks, and he didn't look as thin or haggard. His black hair had been cut so it didn't fall in lank strands on his face, and he was clean-shaven. He looked almost like his old self, like the boy who played air guitar during chapel just to annoy the teachers.

"Dylan! Thank God!" she cried. She was happy to see him looking so much healthier.

He smiled at her pleasantly.

"Do I know you?" he asked.

TWENTY-FOUR

"The past can sometimes blind us from what is happening today," the chief warden said to begin his lecture. "It is why we were in denial about the Silver Bloods' existence for so long. Because our past had told us they were no longer a threat. Because the past had blinded us to their existence. We had forgotten what the early days in our history were like. We had forgotten about the Great War. About our enemies. We had become soft and contented. Gorging on Red Blood and getting fat and lazy and ignorant."

A fine thing to say when your waistcoat strained at the buttons, Schuyler thought. It was yet another Monday. Yet another Committee meeting. A tedious one too, since they wouldn't be practicing *mutatio* today.

Sitting beside her, Bliss and Oliver looked just as bored as she felt. The visit to Transitions had been greatly disturbing to all of them, affecting Bliss the most. Schulyer didn't know what they expected to see, but they certainly hadn't expected to find Dylan's memories and personality erased completely.

Sure, Dylan didn't seem like he was about to knock them out with a mind-blow or start spouting off accusations about one of them being Satan's minion, but he didn't seem at all like himself either. It was as if he were a different person altogether. He was amiable, pleasant, and totally dull.

None of his doctors were around to answer any questions, and the nurse wouldn't tell them anything except that Dylan, as far as she could tell, was "fine." He was dutifully going to all the therapy sessions and making "progress."

Schuyler knew Bliss blamed herself, but there was nothing they could do. None of them had any idea how to fix whatever had happened to Dylan. She had tried to console Bliss as much as she could. She knew how terrible she would feel if she had seen Jack that way. If he ever looked at her as if he didn't know her at all. And yet, that was exactly what was going to happen once he was bonded to Mimi. He would forget about Schuyler completely, forget about what they meant to each other.

Schuyler tried to pay attention to what Warden Oelrich was saying. It was important information, but she had no patience for it right then. Seated right in front of her were the Force twins. She had watched them enter the room together, feeling resentful at the sight of Jack laughing at something his sister said.

Although, of course he had to pretend. The atmosphere at the town house was frenetic with bonding preparations. Different packages arrived every day, and many people came to call. Mimi's bonding planner, Lizbet Tilton, had arrived with a whole crew of photographers, stylists, florists, and "aural-landscape artists" (her exact words for the DJ who was to take over after the orchestra signed off at two in the morning) for Mimi to approve.

Schuyler felt sick just listening to them talk about the event. Not only because the event in question would take Jack away from her forever, but because the way Mimi was acting, you'd think no one had ever been bonded before. The upcoming ceremony did have its advantages—Mimi was so busy that the petty thievery and malicious pranks had finally ceased.

Sometimes Schuyler missed Jack so much she felt a hollow ache in her belly that felt like it would never be filled. She wished he didn't have to hide the way he felt about her. She had to remind herself that it was all an act, but sometimes his indifference seemed so real it was hard to console herself with memories of their private meetings. Sometimes it felt as if her memories were merely fantasies, especially when she saw him in the hallways at school, or when he barely acknowledged her presence in his own home. . . .

Until another book was slipped under her door, a signal that it was safe for them to meet. The last one had been a slim book of poetry. John Donne. That night she had smiled and teased him about his old-fashioned taste. He had asked her what kind of poetry she preferred, and she told him.

Up by the lectern, Edmund Oelrich continued his lecture. "One of the tricks of the Croatan is to use illusion to manipulate its foes.

"You must not fall for the trick of the eye. You must use your internal sight to be able to see what is truly in front of you. Use the *animadverto* and your past memories to make a truly informed decision."

He asked Mimi to hand out papers for that week's reading assignment. Mimi glided around the room passing out the stapled sheets. When she got to Schuyler's table she deliberately knocked all of Schuyler's books to the floor.

"Oops!" she said disingenuously.

Schuyler picked up her books with a frown. She'd had enough of Mimi for all eternity. She wondered how the other vampires put up with it. If she had to spend the rest of her lives dealing with that witch, she would gladly let the Silver Bloods take her.

She was still glowering as she skimmed the reading. Then her eyes widened. At the top of the page she read: *Vampire Bonds, A History*.

Several members snickered out of titilation and embarrassment, and Schuyler found herself blushing. She noticed Oliver paging through the document with a thoughtful air, while Bliss was doodling in the margins.

The chief warden cleared his throat before addressing

his audience again. "I wanted to talk today about vampire twins. At your age, there is a lot of interest in this topic, and I thought I would end this meeting on a more pleasant note. You are familiar with the bond. Each of us has a twinned soul that was formed in our heavenly past. Through the centuries, we spend each cycle searching for our twin so that we may be bound to one another once again in a new lifetime."

All the color drained from Schuyler's face as she listened to the warden's words.

"Sometimes it is hard to recognize our twinned spirit in a different physical shell. Or, as in some lonely cases, one's twin has not been called up for the same cycle again and again, and thus becomes lost in time. There are stories of lovers who have looked for each other in vain throughout the ages, never finding their twin."

Right in front of her, Mimi began to massage the back of Jack's neck.

"However, these are very rare cases. Since there are only four hundred of us, it is not too difficult to find each other. This happy reunion usually results in a short courtship and a public presentation at the Four Hundred Ball. The bond must be renewed during each cycle. Renewing the bond renews the spirit of life that flows in our veins. It is one of the ecclesiastic mysteries. But perhaps the bond is where all the legends about true love and romance in this world come from.

"The Red Bloods even have their own name for it:

'soul mate.' They've taken many of our traditions and practices for their own. Their wedding ceremony is directly derived from our vampire communion.

"Finding your vampire twin is one of the happiest and most fruitful phases of one's cycle. I know several of you have already found yours, and I congratulate you. The bond is an integral part of our lives. It nourishes and strengthens us. We are incomplete without our twin; we are half of ourselves. Only when we find and bond with our twin spirit do we come into our full memories and into our full potential."

Schuyler didn't need to hear or read anything more. She looked over at Mimi and Jack. Saw how the light played off their fair, platinum hair, how beautiful and still and remote the two of them looked sitting together. Saw with new comprehension how the two of them complemented and balanced each other in every attribute: Mimi's glibness softened by Jack's eloquence, her aggressiveness checked by his temper. They were two halves of the same person. A matched pair. Schuyler felt instinctively that there was part of Jack that would always remain inaccessible to her; there was an otherness to him that she would never be able to reach.

She knew that it was rare for twinned spirits to be born in the same family in a cycle, but it was not unheard of, and had been less of a problem in the past, when pharaohs and emperors routinely married their sisters.

In the event that it did happen in the modern age, there

was a spell that kept the Red Bloods from noticing anything strange. Mimi Force would still be Mimi Force after the bonding, except the Red Bloods would assume it was because she was Jack's wife and not his sister. Memories were easily changeable, the truth malleable.

Schuyler saw Jack turn to Mimi with a soft look on his face. For her part, Mimi simply glowed.

All at once Schuyler felt a deep and aching sadness. It was hopeless to think she would ever have a chance of real, lasting happiness with Jack.

There has to be a way, she thought desperately. There has to be a way to break the bond and be free to love whomever you want.

There is.

She started. For a moment she had thought she'd heard Jack's voice in her head. But she didn't hear it again. Still, she knew it had happened. She had not imagined it. She felt lighter all of a sudden, and more optimistic.

There had to be hope for the two of them still.

TWENTY-FIVE

Bliss never understood Schuyler's infatuation with Jack Force and wished her friend would give up that particular ghost. Nothing good could ever come out of it. Even though Bliss was a new member of the Committee and was just starting to accept the ways of their kind, she'd always understood one thing: you didn't mess around with the bond. The bond was serious stuff. Nothing would ever separate Jack and Mimi; nothing was ever supposed to come between them. It was impossible to even think otherwise. Bliss thought Schuyler had always taken it too lightly, which was odd for a girl whose very own mother was the first of their race to break her bond and live (if you could call that living) with the consequences. But as they say, love is blind.

But she didn't say "I told you so" after the lecture. Bliss wasn't that kind of friend. Neither of them spoke as they left the Committee meeting. Oliver had excused himself quickly, leaving before the meeting had even been dismissed, while Schuyler was moody and silent on the walk home from school. Bliss didn't ask her if she still met Jack at that downtown apartment—a secret that Schuyler had spilled innocently one day, several months ago, when she'd told Bliss about the key she'd found in an envelope with an address slipped underneath her door. The next day, when Schuyler had come to school flushed and dreamy, Bliss had put two and two together.

Bliss blamed Jack Force. He should know better. He had access to the wisdom of his past, whereas Schuyler was a new spirit, as blind and dumb as a Red Blood, really. He should have just left Schuyler alone.

Both of Bliss's parents were home when she arrived, which surprised her. BobiAnne usually had her cellulite treatments at this time, and Forsyth was supposed to be in Washington for the week. She put her key in the sterling-silver dish on the front table and walked down the main hallway, drawn by the quarreling voices.

It sounded like Forsyth and BobiAnne were screaming at each other. But Bliss soon realized it was just her vampire hearing that made it seem that way. In reality, they were whispering.

"Are you sure you had completely secured it?" That was BobiAnne, sounding more agitated than Bliss had ever heard her before.

"Positive."

"I *told* you to take it away."

"And I told you that wouldn't be safe," Forsyth snapped.

"But who would take it? Who would even know we had it? He hasn't even realized it's missing. . . ."

There was a hollow laugh. "You're right. He's a wreck. He's finished. All he does is weep and pore over old photo albums, or listen to old tapes. Trinity is beside herself. It's pathetic. There's no way he knows."

"So who, then?"

"You know my suspicions."

"But she's just a girl."

"She's more than that. You know that."

"But how can we be sure?"

"We can't be."

"Unless . . ."

Their voices faded, and Bliss crept up the grand staircase to her room. She wondered what they were talking about. It sounded like they had lost something. Her mind flashed to the necklace she was wearing. She had never returned it to her father after the night of the Four Hundred Ball. But he had never asked for it back either. It couldn't be the necklace, because BobiAnne had seen her wearing it the other day and commented on how well it went with her eyes.

She put away her things in her room and picked up her phone. Dylan had been on her mind all day after the visit. She couldn't believe he didn't even remember her. She didn't know whether to laugh or cry when she thought about him. Bliss changed out of her school clothes and put on something comfortable. She padded into the kitchen, where she found Jordan doing homework on the island counter.

"What's wrong?" Jordan asked, looking up from her books. The kid was in all honors classes—something Bliss hadn't achieved until the vampire blood kicked in.

"Nothing." Bliss shook her head.

"It's about that boy, isn't it? Your friend?" Jordan asked.

Bliss sighed and nodded.

She was relieved when her sister didn't press her to talk about it. Instead, Jordan broke her bar of Toblerone in half. It was Jordan's favorite candy, and she hoarded it in her room because BobiAnne was forever haranguing her about her weight.

"Thanks," Bliss said, taking a bite. The chocolate was sweet and delicious as it melted on her tongue. Bliss was touched. Her little sister had tried to make her feel better in the only way she knew how. "You need help with anything?" she asked, as a way to say she appreciated the thoughtful gesture.

"Nope." Jordan shook her head. "You're hopeless at math anyway."

"You've got that right." Bliss laughed. She zapped the remote toward the small plasma television hanging over the counter. "Is this going to bother you?" She asked, flipping through the channels.

"Nah."

Bliss finished the chocolate and watched television while Jordan continued to work on her math problems. When Forsyth and BobiAnne entered the kitchen a few hours later to rally the family to dinner, they found the sisters still sitting quietly together, side by side.

An emergency Conclave meeting had been called, and at the end of it Mimi was surprised to find Bliss waiting outside the doors. "What are you doing here?" she asked, slinging her gym bag over her shoulder. She'd been in the middle of a two-hour cardio session before heading to the Force Tower. She hadn't had time to change or look presentable. Her hair was still sticking to her sweaty forehead.

"Forsyth picked me up from school, and when he got the summons, he brought me with him," Bliss told her. "What's happened?"

"Your dad didn't tell you?" Mimi hesitated, using a terry-cloth wristband to wipe the dampness on her cheek.

"Something to do with a golden sword?" Bliss asked.

Mimi shrugged without confirming Bliss's guess. She was especially annoyed with Bliss, whom she'd always assumed to be more of an also-ran rather than a homecoming queen in the grand scheme of things. Yet the city's machers and arbiters of fashion couldn't seem to get enough of the russet-haired Amazon. After opening the Rolf Morgan show, Bliss had booked more advertising campaigns than ever. Her face was everywhere—on billboards, on top of taxicabs. She was inescapable.

Mimi would forgive sudden fame and glory—God knows that's what everyone in New York was after—but she couldn't forgive Bliss for choosing sides, especially since it was the wrong one. Everyone at school knew Bliss and Schuyler were *besties*. Mimi found it insulting that Bliss, a girl who wouldn't have had a social leg to stand on in Duchesne without Mimi's blessing, had turned her back on the in-crowd to hang with the ragged little group of misfits.

She didn't want to share her information, but the opportunity to lord her insider status over her former friend was too much for Mimi to resist. "It's Michael's sword," she explained. "The Blade of Justice."

"What about it?"

"It's missing. Charles called the meeting as soon as he discovered it was gone." Mimi had arrived at the Conclave to find her father at the head of the table. Charles had been furious. He was certain someone on the Conclave had taken it, and had begun the assembly by accusing several members of robbery.

Bliss looked around at the Elders, who were leaving the meeting in whispering groups. "Why is it important?"

"Duh. Don't you remember? It's the Archangel's sword. It's only one of two in the world. Gabrielle has the other, of course—you know, Allegra—but no one knows where it disappeared to when she went AWOL. It's been lost for decades. But Charles's, Michael's . . . he kept it in a blood-lock in his study. But someone broke in. It's gone. He's sure the Croatan have it," Mimi explained. The blood-lock was the most powerful security the Blue Bloods had in their arsenal. Only the blood of an Archangel could open the case. It was an impossible puzzle. With Allegra in a coma, there were no other suspects.

"What's it got to do with the Silver Bloods?" Bliss wanted to know, as she sucked on the bandage covering her thumb. She'd woken up one morning to find it bleeding. Odd. Maybe she'd gotten a splinter in her sleep?

"Only an Archangel's sword can kill another Archangel. I can't believe you don't know that, Bliss," Mimi scolded. "Haven't you been doing the reading?"

"But why would Charles want to kill Allegra?"

"Not Allegra. God, do I have to spell everything out? If Lucifer is out there—you know? The High Prince of Darkness? Lucifer's a former Archangel. It's the only thing that can kill him. Normal Blue Blood swords—you get them before you're bonded, by the way, or don't you remember that either? Those just work against any old Silver Blood. But Michael's sword is the only one that can kill Lucifer."

"And now it's gone."

"Yeah. It sucks. Charles is really losing it if the sword slipped from his care," Mimi sighed. It truly looked bad for her father. She could sense that there were members of the Conclave who were suspicious of this "break-in." But why would Charles steal his own sword? Did they actually believe Michael, Pure of Heart, would consort with Silver Bloods?

Bliss looked around for her father. Forsyth was still in the room, probably talking to Charles. "So who do they think stole it?"

"They have no idea; although Charles said Kingsley was the last person who visited him in his study. I know they should never have trusted that loser. Anyway, Kingsley's team is incommunicado in Rio. They couldn't get him on the telepath. And Lawrence hasn't been checking in either. It's chaos," Mimi said a tad gleefully.

"I hope they don't think Dylan's behind it. He can't be," Bliss said nervously.

"What are you talking about?" Mimi asked. "Dylan? Why would he be involved? Didn't he disappear on you a few months ago? He's like, history." Mimi dimly remembered the story of how Dylan had broken into Bliss's window before being taken by a Silver Blood. Bliss had been inconsolable for days, and Mimi had tried to comfort Bliss by reminding her that the monster could have taken her too. She was lucky to be alive. The Conclave had sent a team to investigate and track down Dylan's whereabouts, but the Venators had found nothing.

"Don't you know?" Bliss asked.

"Know what?"

"Dylan's back and he's in rehab."

"Are you sure we're talking about the same guy. Dylan— your deadbeat ex and the guy who killed Aggie? Who got turned into a Silver Blood?" Mimi demanded. Bliss wasn't the sharpest knife in the drawer. A girl who was still wearing last season's sack dresses in May was totally clueless, as far as Mimi was concerned.

"Yeah."

"Why would I know about it?" Mimi asked.

"You're on the Conclave. I turned him in to Forsyth. He said he would let the Conclave know, so that everyone could make a decision. He said the Elders decided to send him to Transitions."

Mimi shook her head, looking mystified. "No. Your dad never mentioned it in a meeting. We did no such thing." She looked at Bliss like she was out of her mind. How strange that Forsyth would keep something like that a secret from the Conclave.

"That's odd, why would he lie to me?"

"Who knows?" Mimi studied Bliss. "Dylan's really back? You're sure?"

Bliss nodded. "We visited him the other week."

"Take me to him. I'll let Forsyth know I need to make a report on Dylan for the Conclave."

Cordelia Van Alen Files
Repository of History
CLASSIFIED DOCUMENT:
Altithronus Clearance Only

Cordelia—
I trust you will find this satisfactory.
Forsyth L.

The Houston Star

BIRTH ANNOUNCEMENT

CONGRESSMAN Forsyth Llewellyn and his wife, the former Roberta Prescott, are the proud parents of a new baby daughter. Jordan Grace Llewellyn was born exactly at midnight on January 1, 1994. Jordan is the second daughter of the congressman. Mother and baby are doing well.

ecause Mimi wanted to see Dylan right away, they decided to visit him the next day, which would mean cutting classes again. Not that Bliss minded all too much. Her grades were the furthest thing on her mind at that point. That evening, Bliss did not ask her father why he hadn't told the Conclave about Dylan. She was wary about letting him know she knew he was keeping secrets from her. Forsyth must have had his reasons, but somehow Bliss had a feeling he wouldn't share them.

The next afternoon Bliss packed Dylan a care package. She knew he was receiving the best care money could buy, but Transitions wouldn't have the newest indie-rock CD or a copy of Absolute Sandman. She thought maybe if he had a couple of his favorite things, it would remind him who he was, and in tandem, what Bliss had meant to him. She just didn't want to give up on him. She'd even decided to stop feeling rejected about what had happened when they'd made out that fateful night. Maybe Dylan freaking out on her was just part of his sickness.

Jordan walked by the doorway and peeked inside Bliss's room. "Are you going up to Saratoga again?" she asked.

"Yeah. Mimi wants to go see Dylan for the Conclave. And his doctor's there today. I can finally ask what's going on with him," Bliss explained, folding a new leather motorcycle jacket she'd had her stylist track down at Barneys and stuffing it into the shopping bag.

Her sister walked in and sat on the bed, watching Bliss pack. "Hey . . . I wanted to ask you . . . you know how you used to have your blackouts?"

"Uh-huh." Bliss nodded, deciding against bringing the teddy bear in a "Get Well" T-shirt she'd bought on impulse at a card shop. Dylan would definitely think it was corny. He'd always made fun of her for having so many stuffed animals on her bed.

"Do you still get them?"

Bliss paused and thought about it. The blackouts used to come with unnerving regularity. She would pass out and wake up somewhere completely different from where she'd begun, with no knowledge of how she'd gotten there. "No. And I haven't had a nightmare in months either."

"That's good," Jordan said, looking relieved.

But Bliss wasn't finished talking. "It's like, I get them

during the day now. Like the other day—I saw this weird thing. I was holding my hairbrush and it turned into this, like, gold snake. Scared the crap out of me."

Jordan paled. "Gold snake?"

"Yeah."

"And the other day I looked up at the sky, and I saw this seven-headed dragon. Freaked me out."

"This happens a lot?" Jordan asked.

Bliss shrugged. "Kind of. I asked Dad about it. He said it was all . . ."

"Part of the transformation," Jordan chimed in.

"Yeah." Bliss finished packing. Her cell phone buzzed. Mimi was downstairs with the car, waiting. Jordan was still standing there, an odd expression on her face. She looked as if she were wrestling with a decision. "What's up?" Bliss asked.

"Nothing." Jordan shook her head. "Have fun visiting your friend."

Bliss hadn't hung out with Mimi for months, and at first she thought it would be uncomfortable between them, but she had forgotten how self-absorbed Mimi Force could be. Mimi chatted easily during the entire drive, talking about everything from her new cast of human familiars, which included the hottest boys from Collegiate and Horace Mann, along with a college kid or two, as well as her plans for the summer: an intensive Chinese-immersion program in Beijing, since she wanted to display language fluency for her Stanford application next year.

"Isn't that funny? Chinese is the only language that isn't in my memories. Huh. I'm staying with Wah and Min, you know those Chinese twins we met at the Four Hundred Ball?" Mimi giggled.

When they arrived at Transitions, Dylan was alone in his room, watching television. "Hey . . . Bliss . . . right?" he asked, turning off the tube. "And you are?"

"Mimi." She looked at him sharply. "You seriously don't remember us?"

"I remember her," Dylan said a little shyly. "She's come to see me a few times."

"I brought you a couple of things," Bliss said, holding up the fat bag of treats.

"Cool," Dylan said, digging into the bag. "What's this for?" he asked, holding up the black leather jacket.

Bliss felt embarrassed. "I . . . um . . . you used to have one. . . ."

"No, it's . . . God, it's great." Dylan put it on. He looked just as handsome in it as the old one. He smiled at her, and her heart skipped a beat. He rooted in the bag again and removed an iPhone box.

"I thought you might want one," Bliss said. "I hope you don't mind. I already programmed my number into it."

"Bliss," Mimi asked. "Could you leave us alone for a bit? I'd like to ask Dylan some questions."

"Sure."

Bliss left the room. A few minutes later, Mimi opened the door. She looked at Bliss with a mixture of pity and contempt. "Well?" Bliss asked.

"It looks like he really has no memory," Mimi said.

"I told you."

"It's amazing. It's like he's a total blank slate."

"You say that like it's a good thing." Bliss glared at Mimi and went back inside the room.

"What did she want to know?" she asked Dylan.

Dylan shrugged. "Not much . . . just a few weird things—and something about jeans or something. I didn't really get what she was after. I told her I didn't even know my name when I woke up."

"You really have no idea who I am?" Bliss asked, sitting next to Dylan on the bed.

He looked down at the comic book he was leafing through and put it away. Then he reached over and held her hand in his. She was surprised and looked at him fearfully . . . hopefully. . . .

Dylan frowned and then finally spoke. "I don't know who you are. But I do know that every time I see you, I feel better."

Bliss squeezed his hand and he squeezed hers back. They sat holding hands for a very long time. Until Mimi knocked on the door to let Bliss know Dylan's doctor was ready to see them.

* * *

As they walked to the main building, Mimi took off her sunglasses and squinted at a figure walking toward Dylan's cottage. "Hey, isn't that Oliver Hazard-Whatever?"

"Yeah," Bliss said. Oliver had told her he might be visiting Dylan after school. Apparently he came up a lot to keep Dylan company. The two of them played chess. Dylan might have lost his memory, but he hadn't lost his ability to slaughter Oliver at the game, Oliver had told her.

"Hold on. I want to talk to him for a bit," Mimi said, heading in his direction.

Bliss wondered what on earth Mimi would want to talk to Oliver about. The two of them despised each other. But they were too far away for her to overhear them.

She did notice that when Mimi returned, she looked extremely pleased with herself, even more so than usual.

As for Oliver, Bliss didn't have a chance to catch up with him. Whatever Mimi said to him shook him up so much, he never did visit Dylan that day.

TWENTY-EIGHT

*S*he heard the car before it turned the corner. A soft purring engine that grew to a massive roar. It pulled up to the alley behind the Perry Street building. A silver gray 1961 XKE Jaguar convertible, sleek and gorgeous as a bullet, with Jack Force at the wheel.

Schuyler slipped inside the car, admiring its classic finish, its silver antique gauges and simple old-fashioned mechanisms. Jack shifted the gears and the car roared up the highway.

They would only have a few hours together, but it was enough—although, of course, it would never be enough.

Each day brought the bonding closer and closer.

She had spied the invitations, and had merited one herself. She'd been surprised at first, then realized it was Mimi's way of letting her know exactly where she stood. The other day she had even caught a glimpse of Mimi in her bonding dress. Schuyler didn't know who was more the fool—she or the girl in the white dress. They were both mad to be in love with the same boy.

Jack was the fool, Schuyler thought, watching him expertly maneuver the car through the thoroughfare. A crazy fool. But she loved him, God how she loved him. She only wished they didn't have to hide, that they could declare their love to the world. The other evening she had told him she was tired of hiding in one place. As much as the apartment afforded an escape, it was also a prison.

Schuyler was longing to be with him somewhere else, even for one night. In answer Jack had slipped her a note that morning telling her to meet him at twilight at the designated location. She had no idea what he was planning, but the small smile that now played at the edge of his lips hinted at a wonderful surprise.

Jack drove the car across the bridge into New Jersey. In a few minutes they pulled into a private airfield at Teterboro, where a jet was waiting.

"You can't be serious." Schuyler laughed and clapped her hands when she saw the airplane.

"You said you wanted to get away." Jack smiled. "How about Tokyo? Or London? Seoul? I feel like barbecue. Madrid? Bruges? Where would you like to go tonight? Tonight the world is yours, as am I."

Schuyler didn't ask where Mimi was; she didn't care and

she didn't want to know. If Jack was going to risk it, then she didn't need to ask.

"Vienna," Schuyler decided. "There's a painting there that I've always wanted to see."

So this is what it's like to be one of the richest and most powerful vampires in the world, Schuyler thought, as she followed Jack inside the Osterreichische Galerie in the Belvedere palace. The museum was closed for the night, but when they arrived at the great entrance doors a gloved security guard greeted them, and the museum curator led them to the proper gallery.

"Is this what you are looking for?" the curator asked, pointing to a dark painting in the middle of the room.

"Yes." Schuyler took a deep breath and looked at Jack for reassurance. In answer he squeezed her hand tightly.

She moved closer to the painting. She had a faded poster of the same image tacked up in her bedroom. The reality of it astonished her. The colors were so much more vibrant and engaging, fresh and alive. Egon Schiele had always been one of Schuyler's favorite artists. She'd always been drawn to his portraits—those heavy, tortured dark lines, the gaunt figures, the eloquent sadness applied as thick as paint.

It was called simply *The Embrace*, and depicted a man and a woman with their bodies entwined together. There was a ferocious energy to the piece, and Schuyler felt as if she could sense the couple's intense connection to each other.

Melissa de la Cruz

And yet the piece was far from romantic. It was fraught with angst, as if the two people in the painting knew their embrace was their last.

There was a melancholy to his art—it wasn't for everyone. In Schuyler's Art Hum. class everyone was enamored by Gustav Klimt's Art Nouveau masterpiece *The Kiss*. But Schuyler thought liking that painting was too easy; it was dorm-room décor, a typical safe choice.

She preferred madness and tragedy, loneliness and torment. Schiele had died young, perhaps of a broken heart. Her art teacher was always talking about the "redemptive and transformative quality of art," and as she stood in front of the painting Schuyler completely understood what that meant.

She had no words for what she was feeling. She felt Jack's hand in hers—so cool and dry, and counted herself the luckiest girl in the world.

"Where to now?" Jack asked as they left the museum.

"Your choice."

Jack cocked an eyebrow. "Let's stop by a café. I have a taste for Sacher torte."

They dined on the rooftop of an apartment building and watched the dawn break over the horizon. One of the advantages of being a vampire was that it was easy to adjust to a nocturnal schedule. Schuyler didn't need as much sleep as she used to, and on the nights when she met Jack, they hardly slept at all.

"Is this what you wanted?" Jack asked, leaning over the small rickety table and pouring her more wine.

"How did you know?" she smiled, tucking her hair behind her ear. He had surprised her by bringing her to yet another beautiful apartment his family owned. The Forces had more real estate than Schuyler had holey black sweaters in her closet.

"Come on, let's go back downstairs," Jack said, leading her by the hand back inside the apartment. "I want you to hear something."

The Force pied-à-terre was located in a building that dated back to 1897, in the prestigious Ninth District, with vaulted ceilings, ornate moldings, and views from every window. It was airy and spacious, yet unlike their sumptuously decorated New York home, the place was sparsely furnished and almost monastic.

"No one's been here in ages, ever since they stopped doing the Viennese Opera Balls properly," Jack explained. He dusted off an ancient-looking Sony cassette recorder.

"Listen to this," he said, putting a tape inside. "I think you might like it." He pressed PLAY.

There was a scratchy hissing sound. Then a husky, low voice—unmistakably female, but sounding ravaged by years of smoking—began to speak.

"It was also my violent heart that broke . . ."

Schuyler recognized the lines. "Is it her?" she asked rapturously. "It *is* her, isn't it?"

Jack nodded. It was. "I found the tape at this old bookshop the other day. They had poets reading their work."

He had remembered. It was Anne Sexton. Reading from *Love Poems*. Her favorite poet reading from her favorite poem, "The Break." It was the saddest of the lot, angry and bitter and beautiful and enraged. Schuyler was drawn to grief—like Schiele's paintings, Sexton's poetry was brutal, honest in its agony. *Love Poems* had been written during an affair the poet had—an illicit, secret affair not unlike their own. She knelt and huddled close to the little stereo, and Jack folded her in his arms. She didn't think she could love him more than she did right then.

Maybe there was part of him that she would never understand, but at this moment the two of them understood each other perfectly.

When the tape ended, they were silent, enjoying the warmth of each other's bodies.

"So . . ." Schuyler felt hesitant and lifted up on one elbow to speak to him. She feared that talking about the reality of their situation would break the magic of the evening. And yet she wanted to know. The bonding was full speed ahead. "The other day at The Committee meeting you said that there was a way to break the bond."

"I believe so."

"What are you going to do?"

In answer, Jack pulled Schuyler down so that they were

lying together again. "Schuyler, look at me," he said. "No, really look at me."

She did.

"I have lived a very long time. When the transformation happens . . . when you begin to become aware of your memories . . . it is an overwhelming process. It's almost like you have to relive every single mistake," he said softly.

"I don't want to make the same mistakes I've made before. I want to be free. I want to be with you. We will be together. I believe I will have less to live for, if I am not with you."

Schuyler shook her head vigorously. "But I can't let you do that. I can't let you take the risk. I love you too much."

"Then you would rather see me bonded to a woman I do not love?"

"No," she whispered. "Never."

Jack held her then and kissed her. "There is a way. Trust me."

Schuyler kissed him back, and every moment was sweeter than the last. She trusted him completely. Whatever it was he was going to do to break the bond, they would be together. Always.

ylan's doctor was a bear of a man, with a full bushy beard and a tilted lumbering gait. Dress him in a red suit and send him down the chimney, Bliss thought, not quite trusting to put her faith in the awkward human, even though he was a very prominent hematologist and came from an old Red Blood family of trusted Conduits.

"My secretary tells me you are friends of Dylan Ward. I know you've been trying to get in touch with me. I apologize for the delay in responding. It's been a very busy week. Someone snuck a familiar into one of the dorms, and it was almost a bloodbath." He winced. "But not to worry, everything's under control for now." The doctor smiled.

"Right." Bliss nodded and took a seat across from his desk. "We're his friends. Thank you for seeing us."

"I'm not a friend. I'm here to find out what's going on with him for the Conclave," Mimi snapped. "I'm a Warden."

He raised his eyebrow. "You look young for your age."

Mimi smirked. "When you think about it, we all do."

"I mean, for someone in your position," he said nervously, coughing and shuffling papers on his desk.

"Get to the point, doctor. I didn't come here to debate the policies of the Conclave. What's going on with that basket case?"

Dr. Andrews opened the file in front of him and grimaced. "Dylan appears to be suffering from a form of post-traumatic stress disorder. We've enrolled him in several regression therapies to help recover his memories. But so far he hasn't made any real connection to anything. He remembers neither what happened to him a hundred years ago nor what happened to him a month ago."

It was just as Bliss feared. Dylan was like an unmoored boat, anchored to nothing and no one. "So he'll just have amnesia like that . . . forever?"

"Hard to say," the doctor said hesitantly. "We don't like to foster false hopes."

"But why," Bliss said, feeling extremely agitated, "why did it happen?"

"The mind does that sometimes; it blanks out everything in order to function. To blunt the force of a recent trauma."

"He's been through a lot," Bliss whispered.

"Silver Blood attack and all." Mimi nodded.

The doctor consulted his chart again. "That's the interesting thing. Like I told Senator Llewellyn, as far as we can determine, there are no signs of Silver Blood corruption in his blood. He has been attacked, yes, and badly tortured, but we are skeptical that he has actually performed the *Caerimonia* on a fellow vampire. He hasn't completed the process. Or let me make it clear: he hasn't even begun it."

Bliss started. "But . . ."

"That's ridiculous," Mimi said flatly. "We all know Dylan killed Aggie. She was fully drained. And he was the only suspect. He even confessed to Bliss."

"He did," Bliss agreed.

Dr. Andrews shook his head. "Perhaps he'd been deluded, or manipulated into thinking he was one of them. Our findings are quite conclusive."

"Forsyth knew this? That Dylan was innocent?" Mimi asked sharply.

The doctor nodded. "I called him as soon as the tests came in."

Mimi laughed a sharp, sarcastic laugh. "If Dylan's not a Silver Blood and he didn't take Aggie, that means he probably wasn't lying when he told me he doesn't know where the jeans she'd borrowed from me are."

"What are you talking about?" Bliss asked, her mind awhirl.

"Never mind." Mimi shrugged. She stood up, and Bliss followed her lead. "Thanks very much for meeting us, doctor. You've been a great help."

Bliss couldn't concentrate. Her fingers shook as she

buttoned her coat. She bumped her knee into the table and almost tripped.

Dylan was innocent.

He was not a Silver Blood nor about to become one.

He was a victim.

For months, everyone in the community had believed in Dylan's guilt in the murder of Aggie Carondolet. That he had dispatched the other victims, attacked Schuyler, and mortally wounded Cordelia. He'd told Bliss himself that he'd done those things. And she'd believed him.

But what if he'd just been covering up for someone else? What if he'd just been made to think he had been infected?

And if it hadn't been Dylan who'd done all these things, then who had?

t was evening when Schuyler left the apartment on Perry Street. Her face was still flushed from Jack's kisses, her cheeks and lips a rosy deep red. Like everything in New York, Schuyler was blooming. A kiss for a kiss for a kiss, she thought, still hazy from their night in Vienna. They had just returned and repaired to the hideaway to shower and change.

Jack had left first—slipping out the side door—and she had waited the requisite half hour before attempting an exit herself.

She was smiling softly to herself, trying to calm her wild hair in a sudden wind, when she saw someone she did not expect to see.

He was standing across the street, staring at her with a look of shock and dismay. One look in Oliver's eyes and she knew he knew. But how? How could he have known? They'd been so careful to keep their love a secret.

The grief etched all over in his face was too much to bear. Schuyler felt the words catch in her throat as she crossed the street to stand in front of him. "Ollie . . . it's not . . ."

Oliver shot her a look of pure hatred, turned on his heel, and began to walk, then run away.

"Oliver, please, let me explain. . . ."

In a flash, she was standing right in front of him. He could run, but he could not outrun her. "Don't do this. Talk to me."

"There's nothing to say. I saw him leave, and then, just as she'd said, I waited a half hour, and then you left too. You were with him. You lied to me."

"I didn't—it's nothing like that—Oh God, Oliver." The sobs forming now, Schuyler felt his sadness and anger wash over her. If only he would hit her, if only he would strike her—do something other than stand there looking so devastated that she could only feel more devastated in turn.

It began to rain. Thunderclouds opened up overhead, and the first raindrops pelted, then drummed on them. They were going to get drenched.

"You have to choose," Oliver said, as the rain mixed with tears that fell from his cheeks. "I'm tired of being your best friend. I'm tired of being second best. I won't settle for that anymore. It's all or nothing, Schuyler. You have to decide. Him or me."

Her best friend and Conduit, or the boy she loved. Schuyler knew one day it would come to this. That she would have to lose one to have the other. That this game would have consequences. That she could not carry on just as she'd had—with a vampire lover and a human familiar, with none the wiser. She had lied to Oliver, lied to Jack, lied to everyone, including herself. But her lies had finally caught up with her.

"You are selfish, Schuyler. You should never have made me your familiar," Oliver said impassively. "But I let it happen because I cared about you. I was worried at what would happen to you if I didn't. But you—if you ever cared about me at all, if you were thinking about me at all, you should have had the decency to restrain yourself. You knew exactly how I felt about you, and you used me anyway."

He was right. Schuyler nodded dumbly as the rain ran in rivers over her hair and her clothes, her garments becoming a soggy mess. Oliver had always been the more sensible of the two of them. He'd had a crush on his best friend, loved her since they'd first met, carried a torch for her for years, but if she hadn't brought the *Caerimonia* into it, hadn't drunk his blood, hadn't imprinted herself on his soul, maybe someday he would have stopped feeling that way about her.

If she had found another familiar, if she had chosen another human boy, Oliver's crush might have faded into a soft, nonbinding affection. Oliver would be able to grow up, love a Red Blood girl, have his own family one day. But she had made him her own. She had sealed his affection with that first tantalizing bite. The Sacred Kiss had marked him as hers.

She had acted selfishly, needlessly, recklessly.

He had no choice but to love her. Even if he left her now, he would never love another; he would always be alone.

He was damned, and she had cursed both of them with her weakness.

"I am sorry." Schuyler's eyes filled with tears. There would be no way to make this right.

"If you are sorry, you will leave him. Jack will never be yours, Schuyler. Not like I am yours."

She nodded, crying bitterly, wiping her tears and runny nose with a wet sleeve. She knew she looked as wretched as she felt.

Oliver softened. "Come on, let's get out of the rain. We're both going to catch a cold." He led Schuyler gently into the shelter of a store awning.

"You're too kind to me," Schuyler whispered.

Oliver nodded. He knew what it was like to love one who did not—or could not—love you back. But he'd had no choice. None of them did.

Venator Martin: They have called for the blood trial. All will be known. I will be discovered.

Charles Force: Yes, I heard. You must be quick. You must disappear. I will help you.

VM: But I want to know why. Why did you have me call the Silver Blood? Why?

CF: Because I had to know.

VM: Had to know what?

CF: If it was possible.

VM: What do you mean?

CF: It should not have worked. (agitated) It should never have happened—it was just a test. To see . . .

VM: What?

CF: No time. (whispers) I know what I must do now.

VM: But the Regis. He will want an explanation for my actions.

CF: Yes. I will take care of Lawrence. Do not worry. He, of all people, will understand why I did what I had to do. Now, listen to me. I am sending you to Corcovado. . . .

ky, you look awful. What happened?" Bliss asked, finding Schuyler standing morosely at her doorway. Schuyler's eyes were red from crying, and she was blowing her nose with a tissue.

"Your maid let me in. I hope that's okay. Are your parents around?" Schuyler asked, still sniffing.

"No. They're at some campaign fund-raiser. What else is new. Come on in. Not that they'd care anyway. You know they like you," Bliss said. As soon as she said it, Bliss realized she wasn't sure if it was true. Her parents had never shown any interest in her friends. They still assumed she hung out with Mimi Force. That's how clueless they were. They'd never even met Schuyler or Oliver.

"Are you all right?" Bliss asked.

Schuyler shook her head. She followed Bliss into her bedroom and climbed onto her bed, leaning back on the pillows and closing her eyes. "Oliver hates me," she said with a strangled cry as she rubbed her eyes. "He saw . . . the . . . two of us . . . Jack and . . ."

"He knows." Bliss nodded. So that's what Mimi was telling Oliver that afternoon.

In answer, Schuyler grabbed a fluffy pillow from among the huge goose-down heap and put it behind her neck. "Yeah."

Bliss sighed. She picked up the television remote and started flipping through recorded programs. "Did you see the latest episode of *The Beach*?"

"No, put it on," Schuyler urged. The fabricated "reality show" about the lives of three vacuous and yet strangely fascinating blond girls from Los Angeles was their favorite.

"So how'd he find out?" Bliss asked, keeping her eyes on the screen. Then she paused the action and turned to Schuyler. "Although, I guess it doesn't matter. You know he would eventually."

"I know," Schuyler said. "I wish you wouldn't look at me that way. I know what you're thinking."

"I didn't say anything."

"You don't have to."

Bliss rubbed Schuyler's back. She was sympathetic, but Schuyler had known what she was doing when she hooked up with Jack. She'd alienated a friend, and for what—Jack Force? What did she see in him anyway?

"Look, I've got to tell you something: Mimi and I visited

190

Dylan today," Bliss said. She repeated everything the doctor had told her.

Schuyler was astonished and confused. "So if it wasn't Dylan who killed Aggie and all those others—who was it?"

"Who knows?"

"Does anyone else know about this? That he didn't do it?"

"Other than Mimi and me? Yeah. Forsyth," Bliss said. She realized she somehow couldn't bring herself to call him "Dad" lately. "Dr. Andrews said he'd called him once the tests came in."

"But your dad didn't mention anything to you?"

"Not a word."

"Or to the Conclave?"

"Mimi said Forsyth didn't tell them about Dylan at all," Bliss said, feeling more and more embarrassed about her father's actions.

"I wonder why . . ."

"Maybe he did it to help me," Bliss said defensively. "He knew the Conclave would want Dylan destroyed, so he hid him from them."

"But Dylan's not a Silver Blood," Schuyler said. "And he never was. So there was no threat that he would be destroyed. They performed the test, and he passed. Hey, what's with the suitcase?" she asked, motioning to the half-packed Tumi rollers at the foot of Bliss's bed.

"Oh yeah, we're going away."

"Where?"

"Rio. Forsyth said Nan Cutler called a major Conclave meeting, told them your grandfather needed help, and now everyone's going."

"What kind of help?" Schuyler demanded.

"Hey—don't worry," Bliss said, seeing the panicked expression on her friend's face. "I'm sure he's all right."

"I haven't heard from Lawrence in a long time," Schuyler admitted. "I've been so caught up with Jack I didn't even notice. What else did Forsyth say?"

Bliss was reluctant to say, but decided Schuyler had a right to know. "I'm not one hundred percent sure, but it sounded like Lawrence was in some sort of trouble."

"What kind of trouble?"

"I wish I could tell you. All I know is this morning Forsyth told us we were going to Rio. Conclave business." She pointed the remote control in the direction of the television screen and fast-forwarded through the commercials.

The show came back on, and Bliss reached under her bed and handed Schuyler a bag of her favorite jalapeño potato chips. "Anyway, don't worry about Ollie. He'll come around. You know he will."

"I don't know about that. I really think he hates me, Bliss. He told me it was him or Jack. That I had to choose."

"And what did you say?"

"Nothing." Schuyler blinked back fresh tears. "I can't choose. You know I can't." She tossed the empty bag and kicked at a pillow. "Everything's rotten."

Bliss kept one eye on the television and the other on her friend. She heartily agreed with Schuyler's assessment. Everything did feel rotten. Like how Forsyth had never been straight with her about Dylan. Sometimes it felt as if everyone was lying about everything.

After a few minutes of watching the main star of the show break up with her boyfriend for the nth time, Schuyler spoke. "You know, I haven't heard anything from Lawrence since he's been there, except that he wishes the weather were cooler. If he's truly in danger, don't you think he would have said something to me? Maybe sent me a message?"

"Maybe he doesn't want you to worry," Bliss said. "He's probably just doing it to protect you. If there's something wrong with Corcovado, he did say he wanted to keep you away from it," she reminded.

"I guess." Schuyler played with a tassel on her pillow. "But it feels weird, you know? I mean, Lawrence doesn't trust the Conclave with anything. Not since Plymouth," she said. "Why would he call for them now?"

"What are you thinking?" Bliss asked. She noticed there was a purposeful look in Schuyler's eye. At least the girl had finally stopped crying about those boys. This was the Schuyler she knew and admired.

"I'm going down there. If Lawrence is really in danger, I have to help him. I couldn't live with myself otherwise."

<<Transcript notes two minutes of tape were lost in feedback. Transcript begins as follows:>>

Schuyler will tell you that I had no choice in the matter. She believes that I love her because I have to, or because I had no choice, but she's wrong. She gives herself too much credit sometimes.

I knew what we were doing, when we did the *Caerimonia*. I knew exactly what it meant. I knew what it would do. More importantly I knew she didn't feel the same about me. I've known that for a very long time. Do you think I'm stupid?

So why did I do it?

I don't know. I wasn't going to. In my defense, I had told her no the first time. We were sitting there in that hotel room, and she was sitting on my lap, and it felt nice, you know. Being so close to her. Yeah, I guess it felt great. I don't want to get into it—I'm not a suck-and-tell kind of guy.

She thinks I've been in love with her since we were kids, or since I first laid eyes on her, or some other romantic crap. But it wasn't like that. We were friends. We got along. I liked the way she thinks. Liked the sound of her laugh. Liked how she dressed—in all those dark layers. What was she hiding from?

Did I think she was beautiful? I'm not blind, am I? Of course I thought she was beautiful. But it was more than that—I liked that she used to wear this ugly shade of blue eyeshadow—girls think guys don't notice stuff like makeup, but we do—and it would get all cakey and smudged at the end of the day. She would have these huge blue raccoon eyes, and she wouldn't even notice . . . I don't know. I was charmed.

But I didn't feel that way about her back then. Not even in eighth grade when we had to go to the Sadie Hawkins dance together and she asked me to be her date, and we spent the evening sitting in a corner making fun of everyone. We didn't dance once, and she wore this hideous, baggy dress. No, I wasn't in love with her then.

I fell in love with her when she found out she was a vampire. Just a few months ago. When she accepted her heritage and didn't flinch from her destiny. Because you know who she's supposed to be, right? I mean, Gabrielle's daughter. Heavy stuff. She's so strong it scares me. I wasn't lying when I told her that.

So, yeah—again, you're asking me why I did it. Why I let her take my blood, let her mark me as her own. Do that whole "familiar" thing. All that jazz.

I don't even know why I bother with these reports. Who's listening to them, anyway?

Anyway, I guess the truth of the matter was, I didn't want her to have to do it with someone else. I didn't want to share. She was already so different from me, changing already. She is different. She's going to live forever, while I'm only going to get to go around once.

I wanted to hold on.

Because yeah, I do love her.

I loved her when she came to me that night at The Bank. When she was looking for me and was so relieved to see me. When she accepted everything I told her, and she didn't even freak out that much when I told her I already knew. That I was her Conduit.

That's why I took the next plane out of the city to

Rio after hers. Yeah, Bliss told me what was going on. Do you think I would let her go there alone? You're kidding, right?

But if you think I walked into this blind, you're wrong. I knew being her familiar wouldn't change anything. I knew that even if she knew I was in love with her, it wouldn't change how she felt about me.

I knew I would lose in the end.

What do I think of Jack Force? I don't. I don't think much of him. Just another guy who thinks he's God's gift to Earth. In his case, probably literally. But, you know—he's irrelevant to me. He just doesn't factor in. Even if they end up together, which I highly doubt given the strength of that particular bond—Mimi is no joke, I wouldn't mess around with Azrael—but even if Schuyler still loves him, or thinks she does, it doesn't matter.

Because Jack is going to leave her one day. I know he will. He's too much for Schuyler. They're wrong for each other. Anyone can see that.

And when he leaves her, I'll be there.

However long it takes, I'll still be there for her.

Waiting.

So I guess Schuyler's wrong. I guess I'm a pretty romantic guy after all.

THIRTY-TWO

*J*ust pronouncing the name of Rio's airport—Galeão— could put one in a Carnaval-ready mood, Schuyler thought. *Gahhhlaaaeonnn*. Now she understood why so many people traveled to this country: even the name of its airport promised sultry and mysterious adventures.

Schuyler, however, felt far from romance of any kind. She couldn't manage to think of Jack without thinking about Oliver. It was too painful. Getting away from the Forces had been easy enough: she just walked out the door. Charles was holed up in his study again, Trinity was away on a girls-only spa vacation, while Mimi was traveling to Rio with the Conclave. Jack was to remain in New York. The other night he had left her another book under the door. A copy of *Anna Karenina*. But she didn't go to meet him. She didn't even have the heart to take the book along with her on the nine-hour flight.

She didn't sleep at all during the trip, and the cramped coach seat didn't help. Schuyler had only ever traveled with Cordelia or Oliver and his family. With her grandmother they had taken little prop planes to Nantucket, and Oliver only traveled first class. She had once thought of herself as a hardy girl who didn't need life's little luxuries, a common enough mistake made by those who've never experienced life's little inconveniences.

The plane finally landed, and Schuyler retrieved her carryall from the bin and shuffled her way to the front of the line. The airport itself was a disappointment, not at all living up to the magical promise of its moniker. The customs and immigration spaces were large and open, but the decor was cold, utilitarian, dated, and institutional. Not at all beachy, sexy, or whatever it was Schuyler had assumed would greet her when she arrived. It was empty and quiet. She'd expected a party, and was met by the Kremlin.

Schuyler understood that the city was considered pretty dangerous, and kept a wary eye. Lawrence was still frustratingly unreachable. The latest messages she'd sent him had been unreturned, and Schuyler couldn't get a lock on his signal. She followed the crowd out to the front of the terminal. Bliss had advised her to take a taxi, but with the little money she had left, she decided to brave it by taking one of the rickety buses that drove down the central areas along the beaches and stopped around the major hotels.

The bus was full of noisy Australian backpackers, and

Schuyler found a seat in the front so she could look out the window. The ride from the airport was confusing, as the highway made various curves and bends, including going through a few tunnels, which left her with little sense of direction. Once in a while Schuyler saw magnificent, moss-covered rock cliffs and hills covered with tropical vegetation, above a coast of yellow-white sand beaches and blue water. She also saw glimpses of the storied favelas—the country's urban slums that dotted the cliffs and hillsides. Evidence of the earthquake's aftermath was everywhere, from the trash-covered lots filled with scavenger birds to the two-story piles of debris that dotted the landscape.

In between the views of mountain and sea she glimpsed towering high-rises, steel-and-glass buildings that were unaffected by the disaster. On the way she also noticed several cars off on the shoulder of the highway, stopped by heavily armed policemen at some sort of ad hoc checkpoint.

Everything was exotic and beautiful and ugly all at the same time. Finally the names on the road signs looked familiar: Ipanema, Copacabana, Leblon. She saw the famous statue of the Jesus with his arms outstretched as if embracing the city, Christ the Redeemer, O Cristo Redentor, on top of Corcovado. She was enjoying the view as the bus chugged along, when its engine suddenly died.

The bus driver cursed profusely as he pulled to the side of the road.

Schuyler was confused, especially when the driver asked

the passengers to disembark along the highway, and to take their luggage with them.

"This again," one of the lanky Australians complained.

"Does this happen a lot?" she asked.

"All the time," she was told.

The bus driver advised them to take a break and come back after an hour while he attempted repairs. Fortunately they weren't too far from the main boulevard. All along the shorefront was a paved walkway with inlaid seashells in a mosaic pattern, crowded with joggers, walkers, Rollerbladers, and strollers. Schuyler found a juice stand nearby and bought a drink. The tropical heat was making her feel wilted.

But when she returned to the designated spot an hour later, the shuttle bus, along with the boisterous Australians, was gone. She was alone. Her annoyance was compounded by a flash of uncertainty when she noticed a couple of young toughs—thin, barefoot guys in faded shorts and holey Chicago Bulls T-shirts walking toward her. They looked curiously at the black-clad tourist. *"Turista?"*

She knew she had nothing to fear, but she didn't want to blow her cover. The boys came nearer. Only then did she notice one of them was holding a broken bottle.

And just when she thought she would have to start defending herself, a shiny black car pulled up. It looked bulletproof, with darkened rolled-up windows.

What now? Schuyler thought she'd only found more trouble.

Then one of the windows rolled down. Schuyler was sure she'd never felt happier to see the boy inside.

"Took a while to find you. Sorry I lost you at the airport. My flight got delayed," Oliver said as he threw open the back door. Schuyler noticed he had two security men in the backseat, and one in the front, including the driver. "What are you waiting for? Get in."

he Copacabana Palace Hotel was one of Mimi's
favorite destinations. She'd traveled to Rio many times
for Carnaval and always stayed in the same corner suite. She
had no idea why Nan Cutler had brought the Conclave all
the way to South America, but she didn't question it. Besides,
it wasn't as if she was going to pass up the opportunity to
miss school.

Jack had expressed no interest in accompanying her, and
she didn't press the issue. Once they were bonded, they
would travel the world together. She missed him, but she was
also excited to be on her own in a new city.

She put her towel down on the chaise longue located on
the private rooftop terrace outside her room. The Conclave
had been invited to dine at Casa Alameida, a villa in the hills,

later that evening. The Almeidas had been part of the Blue Blood contingent that had moved to Brazil in 1808, when the Portuguese royal family and many nobles had fled from, rather than fight, the red-blooded conqueror, Napoleon. They moved the seat of the king's court to the colonies, making Rio the first non-European capital of a European country.

Of course, once ensconced they never went back, and declared Brazil independent, and the prince, emperor. But when the country declared itself a republic in 1889, the Blue Bloods of the city retreated and concentrated on what they did best: building museums and art collections, grand hotels, and encouraging the cultural renaissance.

Mimi admired what the Brazilian Blue Bloods had done with their city, and reminded herself to invite them all to the Spring Gala. The families should really know each other better, she thought. So many of them lived so far away from each other now. Of course the heads of the various Committees would meet with the Coven's Elders in New York every year, but otherwise they had almost no contact with each other.

She lay facedown on the towel and untied the straps to her bikini top.

A muscular pool boy approached, his dark skin and hair striking against his white swimsuit. "Caipirinha?"

"Sure." Mimi pulled herself up on her elbows and didn't bother to cover herself.

His nonchalant gaze—almost obnoxious really, the way he stared at her chest, excited her senses. She was always on a hunt for a new familiar, and when in Rio . . .

THIRTY-FOUR

s far as Bliss was concerned she could stay in Rio forever. All afternoon she'd wandered the city's beautiful beaches, wearing a swimsuit she'd purchased at the hotel shop when the one she'd brought struck her as way too puritanical for this city.

They were staying at the fabulous Fasano Hotel on Ipanema, and although Bliss enjoyed sunning on the roof deck, she'd itched to walk the coast on her own. BobiAnne had asked her to take Jordan with her, and the sisters were having fun swimming in the ocean and people watching. Brazilians wore skimpy bikinis, no matter their shape or size; it was liberating and somewhat appalling at the same time. The American in Bliss believed grandmothers should not wear thongs.

Still, she was really starting to enjoy herself, relaxing in the sultry weather and forgetting they were in Rio for some fairly serious stuff. She'd overheard Forsyth talking to Nan Cutler, and it sounded as if Lawrence was in a real mess. Her parents didn't say anything, but it was obvious they were unsettled and anxious. Forsyth kept snapping at every little thing, and even BobiAnne was on edge. Bliss wondered if Schuyler had any luck contacting him.

Bliss hadn't been able to convince her family to bring Schuyler with them. ("Absolutely not," her father had said. "She is Charles's ward and I do not think he will give permission.") She'd done the next best thing and given Schuyler enough money from her personal account to secure a ticket. Schuyler was probably in the city already, but she was supposed to call Bliss when she got in, and so far Bliss hadn't heard from her. She hoped Schuyler was all right. Rio wasn't a place for young girls traveling alone.

She tried calling Dylan again, but there was no answer. The two of them had gotten into the habit of talking every night and checking in with each other during the day. She knew when he had yoga, when he had therapy, and what time he ate lunch. It bothered her he hadn't returned any of her messages. Where was he?

She dialed the main number of the center and asked for his counselor.

"Dylan?" The therapist's voice was cheerful. "He was checked out the other day."

"Really?" This was news to Bliss. Dylan hadn't even mentioned that he was eligible for release. "Do you know who picked him up?"

"Let's see . . ." There was a sound of papers shuffling. "It says here he was discharged to Senator Llewellyn."

Bliss felt uneasy. Obviously her father had failed to mention any of this to her. Maybe it was time to confront him about what she knew, but the thought of bringing it up with Forsyth made her stomach feel queasy. Dylan would call her when he got a chance, she was sure that he would. She would just have to wait. Next to her Jordan was huddled underneath an umbrella, covered with towels and layers of sunscreen. Bliss mocked her for it—taking out her unease over Dylan by insulting her sister.

"You don't tan either," Jordan retorted.

"Yeah, but I don't care. I like to burn."

"B, can I have a coco juice?" Jordan asked, pointing to a seller who was hawking the frosty wares.

"Sure." Bliss rooted in her bag for her wallet, when everything suddenly went white. She couldn't see a thing. She was completely blind, even though her eyes were wide open. It was the most unnatural, disturbing feeling—almost as if *someone else* were seeing through her eyes. As if there were another person inside her head.

When her vision returned, she was shaking.

"What just happened?" she asked Jordan.

Jordan's face was drained of color.

"Your eyes—they were blue." Bliss had green eyes, as green as the emerald that glinted around her neck.

"You're joking." Bliss laughed.

Jordan looked like she was trying to decide something. Finally she spoke. "Listen, you have to believe that I didn't have a choice, okay?" She grabbed Bliss's arm.

"What are you talking about?" Bliss asked, totally confused.

Jordan just shook her head, and Bliss was shocked to see her stoic younger sister so close to tears.

"Nothing, it's nothing." Jordan sniffed.

Bliss embraced her. "Take it easy, kid."

"Remember that you were truly like a sister to me." Jordan whispered so softly that Bliss wondered if she'd really said it or if she was just hearing things.

"Whatever it is you're worried about, everything's going to be okay, okay?" Bliss said, hugging her sister tightly. "Nothing's going to happen, I promise."

THIRTY-FIVE

*O*liver, how can I ever thank you," Schuyler said, buckling her seat belt. She looked at the armed bodyguards. "Don't you think you've overdone it on the muscle?"

He shrugged. "One can never be too careful."

Schuyler nodded. "Does this mean you're not mad at me anymore?"

"Let's not talk about it right now. We're here for Lawrence, right?"

"Right."

"Did you know the whole Conclave is here?" he asked. "I saw Warden Oelrich on my flight. And the Duponts and the Carondolets are in my hotel."

"I know. Bliss told me Warden Cutler called an emergency session and brought them here. Have they found Lawrence?"

"That's the thing. No one's talking about Lawrence at all. They're all getting ready for a big dinner at some Brazilian Blue Blood's house tonight," he said, as the car drove into the downtown proper, and the landscape became even more scenic: lush greenery, gorgeous beaches, and equally gorgeous people sunbathing upon them.

"Where are you staying?" Schuyler asked.

"The Fasano. The new Philippe Starck hotel. Bliss is there too. I would have gotten you your own room, but they didn't have any more. Do you think you'll be okay sharing with me?" he asked.

"Of course," she said, trying not to look uncomfortable. "Listen . . . about what happened the other night."

"Let's not talk about it right now," Oliver said lightly. "I mean, I was being a bit dramatic, wasn't I? Him or me. Whatever."

"So you didn't mean it?" Schuyler asked hopefully.

"I don't know. Let's just . . . let's just deal with Lawrence first and talk about it later. Is that okay?"

"Sure." Oliver was right. They didn't have time to dwell on that now. They had to find Lawrence.

Her grandfather's continued silence worried her. What if he had been trapped, or restrained, or worse? Had it been wise for him to come to Rio alone? Or to meet with Kingsley's team? Kingsley, who was now unreachable as well, according to Bliss. Schuyler still didn't understand why Kingsley, who'd been shown to be a Silver Blood—albeit reformed—had been allowed to come back as a Venator. Her grandfather wasn't a gullible person, and he must have had good reason to trust Kingsley again, especially after what happened in Venice.

But still . . .

She worried.

She closed her eyes and thought of her grandfather. Pictured his leonine hair, his aristocratic bearing.

The sending was returned immediately.

What are you doing here? Lawrence demanded crossly. He was obviously very annoyed, and worse, sounded perfectly fine.

Saving you? Schuyler sent tentatively.

There was a sound like a telepathic snort.

Meet me at the Palace bar. In an hour.

Lawrence was dressed in his usual tweeds and heavy woolens when they met him at the bar at the Copacabana Palace. His face was red, and sweat was dribbling down his forehead. Schuyler thought maybe he wouldn't complain so much about the weather if he were dressed for it.

"You were supposed to remain in New York," Lawrence said sternly as a greeting. They took seats at the bar and Lawrence ordered a round of drinks. A Bellini for himself and virgin piña coladas for his granddaughter and her Conduit. Even if alcohol didn't affect the vampires, Lawrence liked to abide by Red Blood rules and frowned upon "underage" drinking.

"But grandfather . . . I heard you were in trouble." She squirmed in her seat. She felt relieved that Lawrence was all right, but her grandfather's steely gaze made her recent actions feel impulsive and foolish. More and more it appeared her trip was unnecessary and unnecessarily dramatic.

"That's news to me," Lawrence said, bringing out his pipe.

"But why haven't you returned my sendings then?" Schuyler asked. "I've been worried."

Lawrence sucked on his pipe before replying. "I didn't hear them. I've heard nothing from you until today," he said, blowing smoke into the air.

The waitress returned with their drinks, and the three of them clinked glasses. "There's no smoking here, sir," she told him.

"Of course not." Lawrence winked as he continued to smoke, conjuring a silver ashtray on the table.

The waitress looked confused and walked away, just another victim of the glom. Lawrence turned to Schuyler. "Did you do the exercise as I taught you? Concentrate on locating my spirit?"

"Yes, of course," Schuyler said a bit impatiently.

Oliver piped in. "Telepathic messages are encrypted, right? Could someone have—I dunno—subverted them? Or erased them somehow?"

"That's not how it works," Schuyler said. "They're not

like e-mails sent to a network. Using the glom is a direct line to someone's consciousness. It can't be . . . messed with. Right, Grandfather?"

"I'm not sure. You may have a point, young man," Lawrence said thoughtfully as he sipped his drink. "Using telepathy depends on a vampire's ability to tap into the 'otherworld,' what the humans call the paranormal. The source of our power comes from the great divide, the place where the usual boundaries between the material and spiritual worlds fall away."

"And that's Corcovado; the crossing is here," Schuyler said.

"Yes," her grandfather said, his frown lines deepening.

"And Kingsley? Have you seen him?" Schuyler asked.

"We're in touch."

"So he hasn't disappeared either."

Her grandfather looked puzzled. "No he hasn't. We've been in contact the entire time."

Schuyler shook her head. "It's just . . . we heard . . ." she said weakly. "That you and Kingsley . . . never mind."

Lawrence continued to look mystified as he knocked back his drink.

Oliver excused himself from the table to answer his cell phone, and Schuyler took the opportunity to ask her grandfather something that had been troubling her for weeks.

But the answer was not what she was hoping for.

Lawrence looked directly at his granddaughter, under arched eyebrows. "There is no way. Suppose Jack breaks his bond, there is no recourse for him. It is against our laws. The Code of the Vampires. If his twin invokes the covenant, there will be a trial. If he is found guilty, he will be condemned. Burned. If he chooses to flee rather than face judgment, his own twin must bring him to justice."

Schuyler's breath caught in her throat. "But Allegra . . . she's alive."

"Allegra is practically dead at her own hands. Charles argued that the sentence could not be carried out while she was unconscious. But once she wakes up, she is subject to the laws, as well as he."

"Then why does he keep hoping that she will wake up one day?" Schuyler asked, thinking of Charles kneeling by her mother's bedside.

"Charles refuses to acknowledge the breaking. But he will have to. If she wakes up, the Coven will insist on a trial."

"But you are Regis. You could save her," Schuyler insisted. *You could save Jack.*

"No one is above the Code, Schuyler. Not even your mother," Lawrence said, and Schuyler could swear she heard anguish in his voice.

"So Jack will lose his life one way or another."

Lawrence cleared his throat and tapped the ashes from his pipe onto the crystal ashtray. "If he breaks the bond, even if he manages to escape trial, his spirit will diminish. There is no death for our kind, but he will be fully aware of his paralysis. Fortunately he has never been tempted to break his vows. Abbadon is a flirt and a rogue, but he is loyal at his core. He will not sever ties to Azrael so easily. But Schuyler, tell me, why all this interest?"

"We were learning about it in the Committee meetings is all, Grandfather."

So that was why Jack never wanted to talk about it. Because there was no way to escape the bond. He had lied to her. A lie born of love. There was no hope for the two of them. He was putting himself at risk by resisting it.

Mimi was right. Mimi was telling the truth.

Without the bond Jack would never be the vampire he was meant to be. He would be half of himself, weakened and destroyed. It would happen slowly over the centuries, but it would happen. His spirit would die. And if that did not get him, the laws would. Mimi would hunt him down. The Conclave would condemn him to the Burning. By loving Schuyler he was risking his very soul. The longer they continued to meet, the more danger he was putting himself in.

It had to end.

She thought wistfully of their last meeting. That heavenly evening full of art and poetry, how handsome and brave he'd looked when he spoke about breaking the bond. What he would risk to be with her. Schiele's painting came to mind again. There was a reason why she loved it so much. Two lovers, embracing, as if it were their last. Just as in Anne Sexton's "The Break," Schuyler's story was one of a shattered heart.

There would be no more nights by the fire. No more books slipped under her door. No more secrets.

Good-bye, Jack.

As hard as it would be, as much as it would destroy her very will to even live, Schuyler knew what she had to do.

She had to tell another lie.

A lie that would release him.

Transcript of conversation dated 12/25/98.

Cordelia Van Alen: Come here, child. Do you know me?

Jordan Llewellyn: Seraphiel.

CVA: Good.

CVA: Do you know why I have brought you?

JL: (child's voice changes) I am Pistis Sophia. The Watcher. A spirit born with its eyes wide open, born into full consciousness. Why have you woken me?

CVA: Because I am afraid.

JL: What are you afraid of?

CVA: I am afraid that we have failed. That the battle in Rome was a farce. That our greatest enemy still walks this earth, but I do not know how. You are Jordan Llewellyn. For this cycle you are the daughter of Forsyth Llewellyn. If my suspicions are correct, then you will be our first line of defense.

JL: What must I do?

CVA: You shall watch and listen and observe.

JL: And then?

CVA: If what I fear is true, you must complete what we failed to do in Rome. But I cannot help you. I am bound by the Code. This is the last time we shall speak.

JL: I understand, Godmother.

CVA: Be well, child. Take my blessing on your journey. May it keep you safe. *Facio Valiturus Fortis*. Be strong and brave. Till we meet again.

JL: See you in the next life.

ain.

Searing pain.

As if someone were holding a hot poker to her heart. It was scalding, burning. She could feel her skin turn red, then black, could smell the smoke rising from her frying flesh. This was nothing like the attack at the Repository. She would not survive this.

Bliss tore through the miasma of sleep, forced herself to wake up. *Wake up! Wake up!* It was like being suffocated and torn apart at the same time. But she salvaged what power she had, and gathered all of her effort, all of her strength, and successfully pushed the pain away.

There was a crash and a scream.

She blinked awake and sat up on the couch. She had taken a nap in their suite after coming back from the beach. She was still trying to make sense of what had happened when the door flew open and her parents appeared in the doorway.

In the dark she saw Jordan lying in a crumpled heap on the floor, holding something bright and glittering in her hand.

Her parents assessed the situation quickly, almost professionally, as if they had been expecting something like this to happen.

"Quick, BobiAnne, she's still stunned. Set the spell," Forsyth said as he began to bundle up his younger daughter with the hotel's comforter and blankets.

"What's going on? What are you guys doing?" Bliss asked groggily. Things were happening much too fast for her understanding.

"Look," Forsyth said, removing a small blade from Jordan's hand and tossing it to his wife. "She picked the vault."

Bliss tried to make sense of everything, but logical thinking eluded her in her dizzy and disoriented state. *Was she going insane, or did Jordan just try to kill her?*

She flinched as her stepmother put a hand on her brow. "She's warm," she told her husband. Then she lifted Bliss's shirt and examined her chest. "But I think she's okay."

Forsyth nodded, kneeling to rip Bliss's sheets into strips so that he could tie the comforter holding Jordan closed.

Thinking the pain had come from the emerald stone, Bliss looked down at her chest. It felt as if the stone had burned itself on her skin, branding her. But when she touched it, it was as cool as ever. Her skin underneath was smooth and unharmed. Then she understood. The emerald had saved her from whatever weapon had just tried to pierce her heart.

"She's fine," BobiAnne announced after checking Bliss's pupils and pulse. "Good girl. You gave us quite a scare," she said, tapping her pockets for her Marlboro Lights.

BobiAnne lit a cigarette and sucked on it deeply until it formed a long column of ash. Bliss noticed that her step-mother's face was perfectly made up for a party, and both her parents were dressed in formal dinner clothes.

"What's going on? Why did Jordan attack me?" Bliss asked, finally finding her voice and turning to face her father.

It took a few minutes for him to answer. Forsyth Llwellyn's reputation in the Senate was as of a moderate facilitator, someone who was willing to negotiate with the other side, to bring consensus to warring parties. His smooth Texan charm came in handy during partisan battles in the legislature.

Bliss could see he was turning this charm on her now. "Sweetie, you have to realize that Jordan is different from us," Forsyth said, securing the bundle that held his younger daughter. "She's not one of us."

"One of us? What do you mean?"

"You'll understand in time," he assured her.

"We were forced to take her. We had no choice!" BobiAnne burst out, a bitterness creeping into her voice. "Cordelia Van Alen made us. That meddlesome old witch."

"Jordan is not of this family," Bliss's father added.

"What are you talking about?" she cried. It was getting to be too much. All these secrets and lies, she was sick of it. She was sick of being kept in the dark about everything. "I know all about Allegra!" she declared suddenly, with a look of defiance.

BobiAnne gave her husband a look that said, "I told you so."

"Know what about Allegra?" Forsyth inquired, a look of innocence on his face.

"I found this . . ." Bliss reached into her pocket and showed them the photograph with the inscription, which she kept close by at all times. "You lied to me. You told me my mother's name was Charlotte Potter. But there never was a Charlotte Potter, was there?"

Forsyth hesitated. "No—but it's not what you think."

"Then tell me."

"It's complicated," he sighed. His eyes wandered over to the panoramic view of the beach, not wanting to meet her gaze. "One day when you're ready, I will tell you. But not yet."

It was maddening. Her father was doing it again: side-stepping her questions, stonewalling her. Shielding her from the truth.

"What about Jordan?" she asked.

"Don't worry. She won't hurt you again," Forsyth said soothingly. "We're going to send her someplace safe."

"You're sending her to Transitions?"

"Something like that," her father said.

"But why?"

"Bliss, honey, she'll be better off," BobiAnne said.

"But . . ." Bliss was completely confused. Her parents were talking about Jordan as if she were a dog being sent off to the country. They talked about her like she didn't matter.

But Bliss had to admit to herself that the strange family dynamics weren't entirely new. She thought about how BobiAnne never spoke lovingly of Jordan, had always made it clear that she preferred Bliss, who wasn't even her real child. How her father had always kept an arm's-length distance from his odd younger daughter.

When Bliss was younger she'd relished her parents' indifference to her younger sister. Now she realized it was pathological.

Her parents *hated* Jordan.

They always had.

THIRTY-SEVEN

"That was the hotel," Oliver explained, returning to the table. "Someone's checked out, and a room's opened up. They asked me if I wanted to take it. So you've got a room," he told Schuyler, his face neutral.

"Thanks," she said, trying to make her voice sound as normal as possible, even if there was a hole where her heart should be. But she forced all thoughts of Jack out of her head; later . . . she would mourn later.

"So why is the Conclave here, Lawrence?" Oliver asked. "Is it because of Leviathan?"

"The Conclave is here?" Lawrence asked sharply.

"Oh! I forgot to mention it—yeah. They're here. All of them," Schuyler said. "I think they arrived last night."

Lawrence mulled over this latest piece of information while draining his drink. As if she had vampire ability of her own, the waitress reappeared with another cocktail at his elbow. "More virgin coladas?" she asked, motioning to the half-empty glasses filled with melting yellow goo.

"Make mine a whiskey," Oliver coughed.

"Make that two," Schuyler quickly added, thinking she would risk her grandfather's censure later. "Who's Leviathan?" she asked, turning to Oliver. Around them the bar was starting to fill up with sunburned tourists coming in for happy hour, and a samba band began to play a rousing set.

"If you'd done your reading, Granddaughter, you would know the answer to that question," Lawrence replied.

"Leviathan's a demon." Oliver explained.

"One of the mightiest Silver Bloods of all time," Lawrence said. "The brother of the Dark Prince himself. His second-in-command."

Schuyler shuddered. "But what's he got to do with anything?" She wished the music weren't so loud. The bright, happy sound was in stark contrast to the dark subject of their conversation.

"Corcovado is Leviathan's prison," Lawrence replied. "It is the only place on earth that could hold him. He was too strong to be slain, and was too rooted in the earth to be sent back to hell. When he was captured he was imprisoned in rock underneath the Statue of the Redeemer. Your own mother took him down."

So that's what Lawrence was keeping from her the night he left. Protecting her from the truth and not telling her everything about Corcovado. Leviathan. That visceral hatred she'd felt the day of the fashion show. If she'd paid more attention to her books she could have figured it out sooner. But she'd been too distracted. . . .

"Yes. That was him that evening of the earthquake," Lawrence confirmed. "He is the reason Corcovado is guarded by the Venator elite. We have always kept a strong presence here."

"Now I get it," Schuyler said. "Why you came down here, I mean."

Lawrence nodded. "When Kingsley first brought news of the strange disappearances in Rio, I was a bit unnerved. After the earthquake, I realized I would have to take matters into my own hands and make certain Corcovado remained fortified. I vowed I would not leave the city until I was sure that the threat—if there was one—was completely dis-armed.

"Then a few weeks ago, the Venators confirmed that Yana, the young vampire who'd been missing, had simply run off for a beach vacation with her boyfriend, just as her mother had thought. Meanwhile Kingsley's team brought in Alfonso Almeida, the missing patriarch of the South American clan, after an extensive search in the Andes. Aside from frostbite and an inability to read a map, he was fine.

"So as I told you in my messages, everything was secure. There was no breaking."

"Leviathan?" Oliver asked.

"Trapped for eternity as far as I could see," Lawrence said dismissively.

"But the sending . . . the earthquake," Schuyler argued, trying to talk over the deafening sound of the crowd and the relentless samba drums.

"Mere symptoms in his struggle to break free of his chains. Nothing Leviathan has tried before. But it is of no use. Corcovado will hold forever." He rapped the table with his glass, as if to stress his point.

"So why does the Conclave think Corcovado is a danger then?" she asked.

"Is that why they are here?"

Schuyler nodded.

"I don't know. But Nan must have her reasons; the Regent would never act without just cause." Lawrence finished his drink. "Then again, maybe Kingsley is right," he said softly to himself.

"Kingsley!" Schuyler exploded. "How can you trust *him*? You said yourself, never to trust shiny surfaces. Kingsley's as slick as they come."

"Actually Kingsley has proven his loyalty to the Coven above and beyond the call of duty. Do not speak of him so disrespectfully, Granddaughter," Lawrence said sternly.

"That stunt he pulled at the Repository? That was how he proved his loyalty?"

"Kingsley was only doing what was asked of him. He was following the orders of his Regis."

"You mean Charles *told* him to call up the Silver Blood?" Schuyler half laughed in indignation. Michael was an Archangel. He would never be capable of such treachery.

"There is a reason for everything. Perhaps even for this sudden influx of Elders into this city," Lawrence surmised.

"You know, the Almeidas are giving a dinner tonight," Oliver interrupted. "For the whole Conclave." He checked his watch. "I think it's already started."

Lawrence signaled for the bill. "Very good. Perhaps we will find our answers there. At the very least, the Almeidas throw a wonderful party."

THIRTY-EIGHT

There was a sharp rap on the door, and Bliss noticed how both her parents jumped at the sound. Forsyth took a quick step and looked through the keyhole. "It's all right," he declared, unlocking the door. A stern, elegant woman with a white streak in her raven hair strode into the room, followed by two servants.

Bliss had always been a little afraid of Warden Cutler. The Elder had been the one who had probed her mind for Silver Blood corruption. She still remembered the disquieting feeling of being judged.

"Where is the Watcher?" Nan Cutler asked.

BobiAnne indicated the bundle at the far end of the room.

"You've put her in stasis?"

Forsyth nodded. "Yes. It's going to be a long time until she wakes up."

"We found her with this," BobiAnne said, handing Jordan's weapon to the Warden.

"We need to find a way to destroy it; it's too dangerous for us to use," Forsyth said. "I thought that spell was enough to hold it in the vault, but obviously she was able to disarm it. She's too clever by half."

"If there *is* a way to destroy it," Nan said. "It's not susceptible to the Black Fire."

"You will be able to manage?" Forsyth asked.

"You won't be followed?" BobiAnne wanted to know.

Bliss watched as the grim-faced Warden shook her head. "No, we will not be followed. We will make sure of that. It is amazing she waited this long, really, to make her move. But do not worry, I will make certain that she is no longer a threat to us." She looked with disdain in the direction of the comforter. "Cordelia Van Alen was weak minded as usual to think sending the Watcher into your family would solve anything."

"She suspected, then?" BobiAnne asked.

"Of course she suspected," Forsyth snapped. "You don't give her enough credit, Nan. That bird was sharp. She knew something was up."

"A pity her little assassin was as ineffectual as she was, then." Nan signaled, and her servants picked up the bundle and left the room.

Bliss had no idea what they were talking about, but was desperate to find out. *What did Cordelia Van Alen suspect?*

"We have to hurry," BobiAnne said to her husband. "The dinner starts in an hour."

Forsyth nodded.

"What's going on? Where are you going?" Bliss asked, fighting tears of frustration. "Where are they taking Jordan?" She wondered what had sparked her little sister to do something so crazy. But her parents refused to explain or tell her anything more than the cryptic comments they'd made.

They left for the big dinner at the Almeidas', as if nothing at all had happened. BobiAnne even told Bliss she could order anything she wanted off the room-service menu.

She had to accept it.

Jordan was gone.

Her younger sister, who used to follow her around, trying to emulate her every move. At five Jordan had wanted big curly hair like her sister, and forced the maids to use a curling iron on her stubbornly straight locks, so that her hair would resemble her sister's. Jordan, who had called her "Biss" when she was a baby because she couldn't pronounce her name correctly. Jordan, who'd offered her chocolate and comfort just the other day. Bliss found that there were tears in her eyes.

Bliss understood that she would never see Jordan again.

Why these tears? A low, sympathetic voice asked.

I'm sad.

Jordan tried to hurt Bliss.

I know. But she was my sister. My friend.

What kind of friend brings pain?

Bliss suddenly remembered how she'd felt as if she were being torn in two. She'd experienced more pain than she had ever felt in her life. Jordan had done that. She had aimed for the heart. She'd tried to kill Bliss with that weapon—something bright and golden, like a sword.

But it was different from the sword her father kept in his study. The sword Forsyth had used during the attack at the Repository—when the Silver Blood had killed Priscilla Dupont—was a dull yellow gold. The blade Jordan had used emanated a bright white light.

Nan Cutler had said it couldn't be destroyed, and Bliss suddenly remembered Mimi's words: the Blade of Justice was missing. Did her father have Michael's sword? The only thing in the world that could kill Lucifer? The Archangel's sword? And if so, why had Jordan used it against her? Bliss felt a pounding headache coming on.

I didn't have a choice, her sister had said that afternoon. Why not?

Bliss gradually stopped feeling so sorry for Jordan. She began to feel glad that they had taken her away. Wherever they'd taken her, Jordan deserved to be there. Bliss hoped it was a dark, deep dungeon where Jordan could think for eternity on her crimes.

Excellent, said the voice in the back of her mind. She

recognized it now. It sounded like the gentleman in the white suit. The one who called her "Daughter."

Then once again she could see, but she could not see. She was going to black out. Yes, it was happening right now. She tried to hold on to her vision, tried to fight it, but the same voice inside her head said, "Let go."

And Bliss let go.

She found it was sweet relief to surrender.

imi chose a gorgeous little Valentino cocktail dress to wear to the dinner party. It was a black-and-white strapless confection, with a tight bodice that accented her tiny waist. A thick black band and a dramatic lace bow added just the right hint of girlish insouciance. She had bought it straight from the couture show and brought it to Brazil, because she knew she would have stiff competition from all those Almeidas and da Limas and Ribeiros—annoyingly beautiful Brazilians with blockbuster wardrobes.

She still didn't understand what they were all doing in Rio. Something about Lawrence, of course. And Kingsley, she wasn't sure. Nan Cutler, that wrinkled hag, had been a little vague about the whole thing. But that was the way of the Conclave: they didn't question their leaders. Nan Cutler was Regent, and if she wanted the Elders in Brazil, then the Elders would be there.

A security detail picked her up from the hotel and took her to the sprawling villa. Mimi thought it ironic that while her hosts' massive mansion commanded a grand view of the city, those wretched little huts she saw on the way, precariously perched on the cliff edges, probably had an even better view.

She had expected a bigger to-do, and was surprised to find that only her fellow Conclave members were expected. The Brazilians usually threw massive parties, with samba dancers and festivities all through the night. But the evening was a quiet one, and Mimi politely chatted to a few of the wardens and Alfonso Almeida's intimidating wife, Doña Beatrice, before finding her seat at dinner.

The first course was served, a warm and rich mushroom soup that consisted of a clear broth poured over a mound of mushroom pate. Mimi took a tentative sip. It was delicious. "So Edmund, about our host committee for the spring gala," she said, turning to the dinner partner on her right. She had hoped to meet more tasty Brazilian men at the party, but since none were to be had, she settled for tackling some unresolved Committee business.

"Has the mayor's girlfriend turned you down already?" Edmund inquired, dabbing the corners of his mouth with his napkin.

Mimi grimaced. "We haven't asked. You can't be serious. She's such a frump. Plus, she has no interest in ballet, you know."

Edmund Oelrich chuckled as he sipped his wine, then suddenly began to choke. She assumed his meal had gone down the wrong way when blood began to spurt from his mouth. Mimi screamed. The Chief Warden had been stabbed in the back. On her left, Sophia Dupont was slumped over her soup, a silver dagger wedged into the small of her back.

Then the lights went out, and all was darkness.

This is a trap, Mimi thought, feeling an otherworldly calm as she dove under the table, faster than the knife that was meant for her heart now pinned to the back of her chair.

Silver Bloods!

Of course. But the Almeidas . . . they were from the royal line! How could they have turned?

The fight was silent and swift. There was hardly a scream or a cry, only the hair-raising sound of her fellow Wardens gurgling blood. The Conclave was being slaughtered.

Mimi attempted to collect her thoughts, to remember what she knew, to remember how to fight them. Good Lord, it had been centuries since she had confronted the beasts. Bliss had described seeing a shadowy creature with silver eyes and crimson pupils that night at the Repository. But Silver Bloods could assume any shape they chose, to camouflage their true form.

Mimi bade herself to think, to remember. Her memories responded by flooding her mind with images that almost made her scream. Running through a dark forest, the tree branches scraping her skin, hearing the sound of her leather sandals slapping against the dirt path, feeling the high adrenaline rush of running for her life . . . but what was this, *she* was the one in pursuit. The beast was running *away from her*. She saw the mark of Lucifer on its skin, glowing in the dark.

She returned to the present. Though the room was pitch black, with her vampire sight, she saw Dashiell Van Horn stabbed through the heart, witnessed Cushing Carondolet drained of all his blood, as a Silver Blood held the elderly Warden in its grasp. The room echoed with violent sucking sounds as the predator vampires alternately drank or disposed of their victims. When they were finished the Silver Bloods would take the shape of their victims. The vampire who had been Dorothea Rockefeller was no more. Replaced by a walking corpse with dead eyes.

Too many of the Elders were slow and out of shape. Out of practice. They had forgotten how to fight.

Mimi trembled as she grasped her sword, currently the size of a needle that she'd stowed in her sequined evening bag. It was her only chance to get out of the house alive. But she was outnumbered. She would not be able to cut her way to freedom. Not now. There were too many of them for her to take alone. God, their numbers! Who knew they had so many? Where had they come from? She would have to hide. It was her only hope for survival.

She inched her way out of the dining room to the hallway, picking her way through to an exit. So far she had escaped notice. Until she did not.

"Azrael." The voice was cold and deadly.

Mimi turned to see Nan Cutler standing behind her, holding a sword to her chin. The Warden had lost her old-crone disguise—she looked as young as Mimi, and infinitely strong. Her white hair was a now a burnished gold, and the raven stripe a glossy river of black.

"You!" Mimi accused. But the Cutlers were one of the original seven. One of the oldest and most respected families. Nan Cutler was Harbonah. The Angel of Annihilation. They had fought together side by side during the first inquisition, when Michael had commanded a heavenly army and had decimated their renegade vampire foes. "But why?" she asked, turning quickly and unsheathing her blade, knocking away Nan's sword.

In answer, Nan slashed forward, slicing the air where Mimi had stood.

Her eyes flashed. "You do not have to perish," she said, lunging forward.

Mimi grunted, parrying with a swift counterattack.

"You could join us. Join your brothers and sisters who are still fighting the good fight."

The stupid witch actually thinks I would join their side? After everything Abbadon and I went through to secure this fragile peace we've found on Earth? Mimi thought.

"You are one of us. You do not belong to the Light. It is not your true nature, Death-bringer."

Mimi refused to reply and instead focused on locating Nan's vulnerability. They battled through the room, which was starting to fill with dark smoke.

They're burning down the house, Mimi thought, panicking. Burning it with black fire, the only kind that could destroy the *sangre azul* . . . the immortal blue blood that ran in their veins. Destroy the blood, destroy the vampire . . . memories lost forever. True death for their kind.

Nan cut Mimi's arm with her blade, her weapon finally drawing first blood.

Bitch!

That hurt!

Mimi forgot to feel afraid, and sprung forward with no thought to her safety. She screamed a battle cry, one that came to mind only at that instant. One that Michael himself had used to rally his armies to battle.

"*NEXI INFIDELES!*" she roared. *Death to the Faithless! Death to the Traitors!* She was Azrael. Golden and terrifying. Her hair and face and sword aflame with a blazing, incandescent light.

And with a powerful sweep she cleaved the false Warden in two.

Then she staggered backward. Black smoke was filling her lungs. She had to get out of there. She felt her way to the front door and yanked it open—just as a black-haired man was entering from the other side. In seconds he held a knife to her throat.

Her heart dropped.

The man holding her captive was Kingsley Martin.

The Silver Blood traitor.

This was her doom.

FORTY

*L*awrence had insisted he drive, and as they made their way along the dark curvy highway, Schuyler couldn't help but notice the tiny, flickering lights against the hillside and how beautiful they were.

"Yeah, but they're probably from the slums, which means the electricity infrastructure wasn't set up correctly. And is a potential fire hazard," Oliver pointed out.

Schuyler sighed. The city was rich in juxtapositions: poverty and wealth, crime and tourism in a heady, dizzying mix. It was impossible to admire the beauty without also noticing the ugliness.

They rounded a particularly sharp corner when Lawrence suddenly pulled the car to the side of the road and slumped forward in his seat.

"Grandfather!" she cried, alarmed. She saw his eyes

begin to dart back and forth, as if he were asleep but not asleep. He was receiving a sending.

When it ended, his face was ashen. For a moment Schuyler thought he was going to faint.

"What happened? What's wrong?"

Her grandfather shook out his handkerchief and pressed it to his forehead. "That was Edmund Oelrich before he passed. The entire Conclave. Massacred. Those who were not burned were taken."

"They're all dead?" Schuyler gasped. "But how? Why . . . ?" She clutched his arm. "What do you mean, they're all dead?"

In the backseat she turned to Oliver for help. But he was shocked into silence, his face a mask of helpless confusion.

"The Almeidas were Silver Bloods," Lawrence said, stammering uncharacteristically. "They showed their hand tonight. I had suspected it, which is why I stayed in Rio for longer than I intended, but Alfonso had passed the test. He did not have the Mark. I was deceived." Lawrence was shaking. "But they had help. Edmund said Nan Cutler was one of them."

Schuyler bit her lip.

"Nan Cutler!" Lawrence sounded crushingly wounded. "During the crisis in Rome she had been integral to the Silver Blood defeat. I was blinded by her years of loyalty to the Conclave. This is my fault, I was overconfident and trusting when I should have been guarded and wary." Abruptly

Lawrence turned the car around, causing the car in the opposite direction to swerve wildly to get out of his way. "Kingsley was right—I put too much faith on old allegiances," he said as he floored the pedal and the car shot forward.

"Where are we going?"

"To Corcovado."

"Now? Why?"

Lawrence gripped the wheel tightly. "The attack on the Conclave can only mean one thing: the Silver Bloods are planning to free Leviathan."

They parked at the base of the entrance to the Statue of the Redeemer and ran out of the car. The parking lot was empty and quiet, and they could see the statue lit up by floodlights from below. "Disguise yourself," Lawrence ordered Schuyler. "And you, stay here," he told Oliver.

Oliver began to protest, but one look from Lawrence silenced him.

"I can't," Schuyler confessed to her grandfather. "I can't perform the *mutatio*."

Lawrence was already in the form of the young man with the hawkish nose and imperial attitude she had first seen at the Venice Biennale. "Of course you can," he said, scaling the fence easily.

"Grandfather, I can't. I can't turn into a fog or an animal," she said, following his lead.

"Who said you could?" he asked as they flew up the series of zigzagged stairwells to the statue. Their footsteps made hardly any noise on the concrete as they ran.

"What do you mean?"

"Most likely you are like me. I cannot turn into a cloud or a creature either. But I can shift my features, like so, and take on a different—but human—disguise. Try it."

Schuyler tried. She closed her eyes and concentrated on changing her features instead of shifting her entire form. Within seconds she found she had effectively morphed into one of the rich, pumped-up Argentine *patronas* who were on vacation in the country.

They reached the top of the mountain and stood underneath the statue. Nobody was there. It was quiet and peaceful.

Not for the first time that evening Schuyler wondered if her grandfather was losing it. Weren't they at the wrong place? Why had he brought them here? For what? "Maybe we're too late. Or they're not coming. We should really head to the Almeidas and see if . . ."

"HUSH!" Lawrence commanded.

She shut up.

They walked the perimeter of the statue's base. Nothing. They were alone. Schuyler began to panic. Why were they here when their people were being killed somewhere else? They should go back; this was a big mistake.

She walked around the northeast side, convinced Lawrence had guessed incorrectly. There was nothing to . . .

"Schuyler! WATCH OUT!" Oliver yelled. He had crept up the mountain behind them, unwilling to be left behind.

Schuyler looked up. There was a man in a white suit standing right in front of her, with a golden sword pointed directly at her chest.

She ducked and hit the ground hard, just as Lawrence removed his own blade from a hidden scabbard in his jacket.

The two swords clashed, one golden and fiery, the other icy and silver, the metals ringing against each other, echoing a sound that carried to the valley below.

lood traitor!" Mimi hissed.

"Put down your weapon, Azrael," Kingsley said quietly, still holding his own.

"You will not find me such easy prey as the others," she spat.

"What are you talking about?" he demanded. "I saw the black smoke from the street. My God, what has happened here?"

"You set this up. Don't play the innocent. We all know what you really are, Croatan." Mimi spat, shooting him a look of pure disgust.

"I realize it is hard for you to believe, but I have only just managed to escape from a rather nasty stasis spell myself," he said sourly. "I went to pick up Alfonso for our usual golf game, and the next thing I know I'm trapped in the back of my own car. As soon as I extricated myself I came down here to warn the others."

Mimi sniffed. A fine story Kingsley was telling her. Playing the victim once again. Yeah, right, he'd been detained. When it would have been so easy for him to leave the house from the back and come in the front door.

But what would he gain by keeping her alive? Why didn't he just finish it off? Cut her throat and be done with it?

"Where's Lawrence?" Kingsley coughed as several explosions shook the ground beneath them. "I tried sending him a message, but I couldn't find him in the glom."

"He's not here," Mimi said, noticing that Kingsley had lowered his dagger. She could kill him now, while he was unguarded. But what if he was telling the truth? Or was his act just another part of the trap?

Before she could make a decision, there was a crash, and Forsyth Llewellyn appeared. He was carrying the limp body of his wife. His clothes were singed, and he sported a deep gash on his forehead. So he had survived as well. Mimi felt a little better. Maybe there were more survivors. But where had the Silver Bloods gone? After she had felled Nan Cutler, the rest of them seemed to have disappeared in the smoke.

"Everyone else is dead," Mimi told Forsyth. "You and I

are the only ones left. I saw Edmund fall, Dashiell, Cushing . . . everyone. The Regent."

"Nan's dead?" Forsyth Llewellyn asked, aghast.

"She was one of them," Mimi told him, her eyes watering from the smoke. "I killed her myself."

"You . . ."

"C'mon, we've got to get out of here," Kingsley said, suddenly pulling the two of them out of the doorway, which crashed to the ground in flames.

If Kingsley wanted her dead, he sure wasn't acting like it.

"Thanks," she said, tucking her sword—again the size of a needle—back into her bag, which she miraculously found she was still holding.

Kingsley didn't reply, his face hardening as he looked above her shoulder. Meanwhile, Forsyth Llewellyn looked utterly lost, sitting in the middle of the street with his head in his hands.

Mimi turned to where Kingsley was looking. The grand eighteenth-century villa was now a giant black fireball. It was a crematorium. The Silver Bloods were back. And they had struck deep into the heart of the Coven.

The Second Great War had begun.

FORTY-TWO

From far away, Schuyler heard the sound of grunts and screams, the clanging of metal against metal.

Wake up.

Wake up, child.

There was a voice inside her head. A sending.

A voice she had heard before.

She opened her eyes. Her mother stood before her. Allegra Van Alen was clad in white raiments, and she held a golden sword in her hands. *For me?*

What was once mine is rightfully yours.

Stunned, Schuyler took the sword. Once she did, the image of her mother disappeared. *Allegra . . . Come back . . .* Schuyler thought, suddenly afraid. But a desperate yell from Oliver brought her back to the present.

She looked up and saw Lawrence locked in a fierce struggle with his adversary. His sword fell to the ground. Above him loomed the white, shining presence. It was so bright it was blinding, like looking into the sun. It was the Lightbringer. The Morningstar.

Her blood froze.

Lucifer.

"Schuyler!" Oliver's voice was hoarse. "Kill it!"

Schuyler raised her mother's sword, saw it glinting in the moonlight, a long, pale, deadly shaft. Raised it in the direction of the enemy. Ran with all her might and thrust her weapon toward its heart.

And missed.

But she had given Lawrence time to regain his weapon, and it was his blade that found its mark, slicing into the enemy's chest and spilling blood everywhere.

They had won.

Schuyler sank to the ground in relief.

But then came a great crack in the sky, the sound of the heavens splitting open, the roaring, deafening sound of thunder. Then the statue was broken in two. Its very foundations shattered. There was a deep rumble, and the ground underneath them began to shake and split into two.

"What's happening?" Schuyler screamed.

A dark flame burst from the earth, and a mighty demon with crimson eyes and silver pupils leaped into the sky. It laughed a deep booming laugh, and with its blazing spear, pinned Lawrence to the ground, where he lay.

FORTY-THREE

The demon disappeared. The mist lifted, and Schuyler staggered over to where her grandfather had fallen. To where he lay so still, his eyes wide open. "Grandfather . . ." Schuyler cried. "Oliver, do something!" she said as she tried to staunch the flow of dark sapphire blood that spilled from the open wound, the gaping, corrugated hole in the middle of Lawrence's chest.

"It's too late," Oliver whispered, kneeling by Lawrence's side.

"What do you mean? No . . . let's get a vial . . . for the next cycle. Take it to the clinic."

"Leviathan's spear is poisoned. It will corrode the blood," Oliver said. "It has the black fire in it. He is gone." His handsome face was drawn with sorrow.

"No!" Schuyler screamed, tears streaming down her cheeks.

There was a moan from the far side of the mountain, and they turned to find the shape of the man in the white suit begin to change. His features softened, faded, and the golden man disappeared to reveal an ordinary boy in a black leather jacket.

A boy with black hair.

"That is no Silver Blood," Oliver said.

"He must have been possessed," Schuyler said, her voice breaking a little while Oliver walked over to gently close Dylan's eyes. Schuyler noticed there were tears in Oliver's eyes as well as her own.

"Yes." He nodded.

"The blankness . . . it was the *alienari*," Schuyler said, realizing how deeply they had been deceived.

"An old Silver Blood trick." Oliver nodded. "Disguised as Lucifer himself, so that Lawrence would kill his own kind. An innocent."

Schuyler nodded. "I sensed it, Oliver—Lawrence must have too. There was something wrong. The light was blinding, you couldn't even look at him directly. It was a distraction, so that we wouldn't be able to see what was in front of us. The image of Lucifer was so powerful, it threw us off. I should have used the *animaverto*."

"This was a well-executed plan. Leviathan was freed by Dylan's death. The prison bonds can only be broken when a Blue Blood commits the highest crime of all—murder of their own kind. It's in the books," Oliver said.

"Grandfather," Schuyler said softly, taking Lawrence's hand in hers. They'd had too little time together; there was so much she still had to learn. So much he still had to teach her.

Then for the last time, she heard Lawrence's voice inside her head.

Listen.

I was not worthy of this task. I have learned nothing over the centuries. I did not find the Dark Prince. I am no keeper. You must ask Charles . . . you must ask him about the Gates . . . about the Van Alen legacy and the Paths of the Dead. There has to be a reason why the Silver Bloods have been able to so easily breach the divisions between the worlds.

"What gates? What paths?"

You are Allegra's daughter. Your sister will be our death. But you are our salvation. You must take your mother's sword and slay him. I know you will triumph.

Then Lawrence spoke no more.

FORTY-FOUR

Dark blood. There was blood everywhere. On her face. In her eyes. On her hands. On her clothes. Then slowly it began to vanish, the metallic tinge turned white and invisible as the cold night air hit the liquid. Vampire blood . . .

Bliss stared at her arms.

What happened?

She couldn't remember. She had blacked out.

Or had she?

The memories began to flood back.

She saw herself get inside the car with her parents, saw them nod at her. They were expecting her to accompany them. How strange. It was like being in a movie. She could see out of her eyes, but she could not move her arms or legs or even speak. Someone else was doing that for her.

Someone else was inside her body.

The man in the white suit.

Yes.

I am you. You are me. We are one, my daughter.

They arrived at a hilltop mansion, and Bliss remembered hiding in the shadows until the time came. She had watched the killing unfold with an overwhelming sense of horror. The massacre she had inflicted with her own hands. She had been imprisoned in her own body, a helpless figure, trapped inside her head while the other took over. Inside she had raged and wept and screamed. But she was powerless, with absolutely no ability to stop herself.

Slowly, she began to remember what happened during her blackouts. Began to realize the truth.

She was the one who had attacked Dylan that first night at The Bank. She had wanted to drain him, but something—a vestigial attraction to him—had stopped her, so she had taken Aggie instead. She had attempted to take Schuyler twice. That was why Schuyler's bloodhound had barked at her—Beauty knew her true nature even if Schuyler did not. Then she had attacked Cordelia, had almost taken her, if Dylan had not stopped her.

Dylan had been a problem. He knew but did not know. That was why his memory was so screwed up all the time. He knew the truth even though she'd tried to wipe it from his consciousness.

That first time he had returned to warn her about the Silver Bloods had resulted in that bloody scene in the bathroom. She remembered his blood-soaked leather jacket, the scratches on her face and the bruise on her neck. But he had escaped, and she'd had to send others to track him down. But the Venators got to him first. Oliver was wrong. They were not Silver Bloods. They had let Dylan go when they discovered he was innocent.

He was free to return to her.

The stupid, stupid boy.

"I know who the Silver Blood is," Dylan had said that night he crashed through the window. "It's you."

And right then and there, she had changed his memory. Made him think it was Schuyler.

A small, sad voice inside her began to cry.

I loved him. I loved Dylan.

We love no one.

No one but ourselves.

Forsyth had known all along. That's why she could never bring herself to ask him about Dylan, because somewhere in her subconscious she knew the reason why her father was keeping things from her. Because part of her could not accept who she really was.

She watched as she left the burning house, taking a car that had a body stuffed in the trunk. Dylan. She had taken him to the mountaintop, where Lawrence and Schuyler were waiting. Taken him to Corcovado, where he would be a sacrifice. There, she had shaped him in his image.

She had brought him to his death.

It was Lawrence's blade that struck, but it was she who had killed him.

As she had killed so many others.

She heard the voices of everyone she had taken. They were all there, inside her head, screaming, crying.

SILENCE!

Nan Cutler was part of it, she realized. Nan was the Warden who had checked for the Mark of Lucifer on her neck. She'd been the one who had cleared Bliss of suspicion during the investigation. Bliss suddenly had an idea, and lifted her hair from her neck and touched her fingers to her skin. She felt it at once. She turned to the mirror and saw it. A small star-shaped scar that branded her as the devil's own.

But why? the small, sad voice asked.

Is that the one who calls herself "Bliss." Is she still there?

Yes, said the same tiny voice. It was the voice of Bliss Llewellyn. The same voice of Maggie Stanford before her. It was always the same way. Every cycle. They never wanted to accept the truth of their heritage.

I did not know.

I do not want this.

Your desires are immaterial. Now pick yourself up and walk toward your friends. Not everything went to plan. Some of us were killed. We must bide our time again.

I know who you are now, "Bliss" said.

You are Lucifer.

Lightbringer.

Morningstar.

The former Prince of Heaven.

Her true and immortal father.

awrence was dead. Schuyler felt as if her heart would shatter from the loss of her beloved grandfather. How was this allowed to happen? What had he been talking about? Her sister? Who? What?

The first rays of dawn lit the mountaintop. A figure walked up the steps.

"Someone's coming," Oliver warned.

"It's just Bliss," Schuyler said as their friend reached them. "Thank God you're okay."

"My sister is dead. My stepmother too. I don't know where my father is," Bliss said in a flat, strangled voice. "There was black smoke. The Conclave . . . they've been . . . What's happened here?" she asked, seeing the prone bodies of Lawrence and Dylan on the ground.

"Is that? Oh my God!"

Schuyler grabbed Bliss by the waist and let her sob on her shoulder. "I'm so, so sorry."

Bliss removed herself from Schuyler's embrace and knelt by the body of the boy she loved. She cradled him in her arms, and her tears fell on his cheeks. "Dylan . . . no," she whispered. "No."

"There was nothing we could do . . . it was a mistake," Schuyler said, trying to explain. "Lawrence . . ."

But Bliss wasn't listening. She wiped away her tears on her sleeve. "I'll take him down," she said, putting her arms around him, lifting him up. He was so light, he was almost insubstantial. It was like holding air. There was nothing left of him. She made her way down the mountain alone, hic-cupping sobs.

Schuyler watched them with tears falling from her own eyes. She had not been able to save Dylan. She had lost two friends today.

"It will be all right, you'll see," Oliver said, kneeling to cover the wound on her arm with a torn strip from his shirt.

Schuyler looked at him. Saw the sad, drawn expression on his handsome face, his dark caramel hair falling over his wounded forehead. Kind, gentle, wonderful Oliver. The enormity of her deception struck her. She had deceived them both in her words and actions. Because she did love him. Had always loved him. Loved Oliver and Jack both. They were both part of her. She had denied her love for

Oliver in order to allow herself to love Jack. But now so much was clear.

"I love you," she said.

"I know." Oliver smiled and continued to bandage her arm.

EPILOGUE

Two Weeks Later

So this was their sordid little love nest. Mimi let herself into the dark apartment. She had found a key that she'd never seen before in Jack's room. She had suspected where it led, and she knew he wouldn't be long in coming.

The door opened silently, and Jack entered.

The look on her brother's face told her all she needed to know. Mimi smiled to herself. So the little half-blood finally cut her ties.

"You've won," Jack said softly. He looked at Mimi with such fiery hatred that she almost cowered at his words. But she was no weakling. She was Azrael, and Azrael did not cower, not even to Abbadon.

"I've won nothing," Mimi replied coldly. "Please remember that almost all of the Elders are dead, that the Dark

Prince is ascendant, and what is left of the Conclave is being led by a broken man who used to be the strongest of us all. And yet all you seem to care about, my darling, is that you no longer get to play with your little love toy."

Instead of answering her, Jack flew across the room and slapped her hard across the face, sending her crashing to the floor. But before he could wield another blow, Mimi leaped up and slammed him against the window, knocking him completely out of breath.

"Is this what you want?" she hissed as she lifted him up by his shirt collar, his face turning a ghastly shade of red.

"Don't let me destroy you," he sneered.

"Just try, my sweet."

Jack twisted out of her grasp and flipped her over, kicking her down the length of the room. She sprung up with her hands clenched, her nails sharp as claws, and fangs bared. They met halfway in the air, and Jack put a hand on her throat and began to squeeze. But she scratched at his eyes and wrenched her body so that she was rolling on top of him, her sword at his throat, with the upper hand.

SUBMIT. Mimi sent.

NEVER.

You are mine.

You are wrong.

Mimi threw him across the room. Both of them were bruised and bloody. Mimi's blouse was ripped in half, and Jack's shirt was torn at the collar.

Jack attacked again—this time pinning Mimi to the ground. His breath was hot in her ear. She could feel his body tense, rigid, and pulsing on top of hers, could almost see the red aura of his rage.

"You want this," she said slyly. "You want me."

"No."

"Yes."

He twisted her arms behind her back, pinned his knees against her hips, then tightened his grip on her wrists so that they grew purple with bruises. For weeks, the shape of his fingers would be imprinted on her flesh.

For a moment she was truly terrified. This was Abbadon the Cruel. The Angel of Destruction. He could and would destroy her if he had to. If he felt like it. He had destroyed worlds before. He had decimated Paradise in the name of the Morningstar.

She trembled in his grasp.

All his gentleness, all his kindness, all the bright shining gorgeousness of his love, he had always given to someone else. He had adored Gabrielle, had worshipped her, had written her poems and sang her songs, and for Schuyler there were novels and love notes and sweet kisses and furtive tender meetings by a fireplace.

But for his twin, Azrael, he had shown nothing but his anger and violence. His strength and destruction.

He saved the best of himself for those who did not deserve it. Never showed his true face to those damnable Daughters of the Light.

For Azrael, there was only darkness and annihilation.

Rape and carnage.

War and pillage.

A tear escaped from her eye and glittered in the moonlight.

But just as Mimi thought he would destroy her forever, Jack began kissing her with such force that her lips and neck would be sore and swollen with his bites. In answer, she pulled him toward her, as hard as she could, by the roots of his hair.

Love. It's so close to hate, it's almost indistinguishable.

But this is how it was for the two of them.

Love and hate.

Life and death.

Joy and anguish.

Finally he lay still against her, drifting into a dreamless sleep. She smoothed his hair from his brow and called his name softly. Abbadon the Unlikely. Named so because his wistful nature masked a cold and fierce rage.

The Destroyer of Worlds, and the emperor of her own heart.

One day he would thank her for saving his life.

Acknowledgments

Thank you to everyone who helped make this book a reality, most of all my wonderful husband (and defacto editor/cocreator), Mike Johnston, who comes up with all the brilliant ideas; my superbly awesome editor, Jennifer Besser; and everyone at Hyperion, who have been huge champions of the series, especially Jennifer Corcoran, Angus Killick, Nellie Kurtzman, Colin Hosten, Dave Epstein, and Elizabeth Clark (thank you for the amazing covers!).

Thank you to Alicia Carmona, for all the awesome Brazil research. Much love to my insanely supportive family, the DLCs and Johnstons, especially Christina Green and Alberto de la Cruz, who are not just related to me but also keep the "Office of Melissa de la Cruz" in working order. Thank you to my agents, Richard Abate, Richie Kern, Melissa Myers, and everyone at Endeavor, for all your hard work on my behalf. Thank you also to Kate Lee and Larissa Silva at ICM, for all your support.

Most of all I'd like to thank my readers, who mean the world to me. Thank you for sharing your thoughts, dreams, and questions in e-mails or on the Web site. Thank you to the fabulous Amanda, who runs the awesome Blue Bloods message boards; and to everyone who has made a fan site, role-playing game, or online group devoted to the series. You all rock so hard it hurts.

The story continues in

the Van Alen Legacy

Book Four of
Blue Bloods

Turn the page for an exciting preview . . .

here had been little time to mourn. Upon returning to New York after Lawrence's murder in Rio (covered up by the Committee with a proper obituary in the *Times*), Schuyler Van Alen had been on the run. No rest. No respite. A year of constant motion, barely one step ahead of the Venators hunting her. A flight to Buenos Aires followed by one to Dubai. A sleepless night in a youth hostel in Amsterdam followed by another in a bunk bed in an auditorium in Bruges.

She had marked her sixteenth birthday aboard the Trans-Siberian Railway—celebrating with a cup of watery Nescafé coffee and several crumbly Russian tea cookies. Somehow, her best friend, Oliver Hazard-Perry, had found a candle to light in one of the *suharkies*. He took his job as human Conduit pretty seriously. It was thanks to Oliver's careful accounting that they had been able to stretch their money so far. The Conclave had frozen his access to the well-funded Hazard-Perry accounts as soon as they had left New York.

Now it was August in Paris, and hot. They had arrived to find most of the city a ghost town: bakeries, boutiques, and bistros shuttered while their proprietors absconded to three-week vacations in the beaches up north. The only people around were American and Japanese tourists, who mobbed every museum gallery, every garden in every public square, inescapable and ubiquitous in their white sneakers and baseball caps. But Schuyler welcomed their presence. She hoped the slow-moving crowds would make it easier for her and Oliver to spot their Venator pursuers.

Schuyler had been able to disguise herself by changing her physical features, but performing the *mutatio* was taking a toll on her. She didn't say anything to Oliver, but lately she couldn't even do so much as change the color of her eyes.

And now, after almost a year of hiding, they were coming out into the open. It was a gamble, but they were desperate. Living without the protection and wisdom of the secret society of vampires and their select group of trusted humans had taken its toll. And while neither of them would ever admit it, they were both tired of running.

So for now Schuyler was seated in the back of a bus, wearing a pressed white shirt buttoned to the neck over slim black pants and flat black shoes with rubber soles. Her dark hair was pulled back in a ponytail, and except for a hint of lip gloss, she wore no makeup. She meant to blend in with the rest of the catering staff who had been hired for the evening.

But surely someone would notice. Surely someone would hear how hard her heart was beating, would remark on how her breathing was shallow and quick. She had to calm down. She had to clear her mind and become the blasé contract caterer she was pretending to be. For so many years Schuyler had excelled at being invisible. This time, her life depended on it.

The bus was taking them over a bridge to the Hôtel Lambert on the Île Saint-Louis, a small island on the Seine River. The Lambert was the most beautiful house in the most beautiful city in the world. At least, she had always thought so. Although "house" was putting it mildly. "Castle" was more like it, something out of a fairy tale, its massive river walls and gray mansard roofs rising from the surrounding mist. As a child she had played hide-and-seek in the formal gardens, where the conical sculpted trees reminded her of figures on a chessboard. She remembered staging imaginary productions inside the grand courtyard and throwing bread crumbs to the geese from the terrace overlooking the Seine.

How she had taken that life for granted! Tonight she would not enter the hotel's exclusive, exalted domain as an invited guest, but rather as a humble servant. Like a mouse creeping into a hole. Schuyler was anxious by nature, and she needed almost all her self-control to keep it together. At any moment she feared she might scream—she was already so nervous she couldn't stop her hands from trembling. They vibrated, fluttering in her lap like trapped birds.

Next to her, Oliver was handsome in a bartender's uniform, a tuxedo with a black silk bow tie and silver shirt studs. But he was pale beneath his butterfly collar, his shoulders tense under a jacket that was a little too big. His clear hazel eyes were clouded, looking more gray than green. Oliver's face did not display the same blank, bored look as the others'. He was alert, ready for a fight or flight. Anyone who looked at him long enough could see it.

We shouldn't be here, Schuyler thought. What were we thinking? The risk is too great. They're going to find us and separate us . . . and then . . . well, the rest was too horrible to contemplate.

She was sweating under her starched shirt. The air-conditioning wasn't working, and the bus was packed. She leaned her head against the windowpane. Lawrence had been dead for over a year now. Four hundred forty-five days. Schuyler kept count, thinking that maybe once she hit a magical number, it would stop hurting.

This was no game, although sometimes it felt like a horrid, surreal version of cat and mouse. Oliver put a hand on top of hers to try and stop her hands from shaking. The tremors had begun a few months ago, just a slight twitching, but soon she realized she had to concentrate whenever she

did something as simple as pick up a fork or open an envelope.

She knew what it was, and there was nothing she could
do about it. Dr. Pat had told her the first time she visited her
office: she was the only one of her kind, *Dimidium Cognato*, the
first half-blood, and there was no telling how her human
body would react to the transformation into immortal; there
would be side effects, obstacles particular to her case.

Still, she felt better once Oliver held her hand in his.
He always knew what to do. She depended on him for so
much, and her love for him had only deepened in the year
they had spent together. She squeezed his hand, intertwined
her fingers around his. It was his blood that ran through her
veins, his quick thinking that had secured her freedom.

As for everyone and everything they had left behind in
New York, Schuyler did not dwell on it anymore. All of that
was in the past. She had made her choice and was at peace
with it. She had accepted her life for what it was. Once in a
while she missed her friend Bliss very keenly, and more than
once wanted to get in touch with her, but that was out of the
question. No one could know where they were. No one. Not
even Bliss.

Maybe they would be lucky tonight. Their luck had
held so far. Oh, there had been a few close calls here and
there—that one evening in Cologne when she'd abruptly run
from a woman who had asked for directions to the cathedral.
Illuminata had given the agent away. Schuyler had caught

that soft imperceptible glow in the twilight before booking as fast as she could. Disguises only went so far. At some point, your true nature revealed itself.

Wasn't that what the Inquisitor had argued during the official investigation into the events in Rio? That maybe Schuyler wasn't who she was supposed to be?

Outlaw. Fugitive. That's what she was now. Certainly not Lawrence Van Alen's grieving granddaughter.

No.

According to the Conclave, she was his killer.

*O*h, gross! She'd stepped in something icky. Beyond icky. It squished beneath her foot—a wet, gasping sound. Whatever it was, it was sure to ruin her pony-hair boots. What was she doing wearing pony-hair boots to a reconnaissance mission anyway? Mimi Force lifted her heel and assessed the damage. The zebra pattern was stained with something brown and leaky.

Beer? Whiskey? A combination of all the bottom-shelf alcohol they served in this place? Who knew? For the umpteenth time this year, she wondered why on earth she'd ever signed up for this assignment. It was the last week of August. By all rights she should be on a beach in Capri, working on her tan and her fifth limoncello. Not creeping around some honky-tonk bar in the middle of the country. Somewhere between the dust bowl and the rust belt—or was it the rust bowl and the dust belt? Wherever they were, it was a sleepy, sad little place, and Mimi couldn't wait to leave it.

"What's wrong?" Kingsley Martin nudged her. "Shoes too tight again?"

"Will you leave me alone?" she sighed, moving away from him, making it clear she found the alcove they were hiding in too close quarters. She was tired of his teasing. Especially since, to her complete and utter horror, she discovered she was starting to like it. That was simply unacceptable. She *hated* Kingsley Martin. After everything that he'd done to her, she couldn't see how she could feel otherwise.

"But where's the fun in that?" He winked. The most infuriating thing about Kingsley—other than the fact that he had once tried to bring about her demise—was that somewhere between chasing down leads on the beaches of Punta del Este or through the skyscrapers of Hong Kong, Mimi had started to find him . . . attractive. It was enough to make her stomach turn. "C'mon, Force, lighten up. You know you want me," he said with a smug smile.

"Oh my god!" she huffed, turning around so that her long blond hair whipped over her shoulder and hit him square in the face. *"As if!"* He might be faster and stronger than she was—the big man on the Venator team, and for all intents and purposes her boss—but really *she* should be the one leading them, as she outranked him in the Conclave hierarchy. If you could call that sorry group of cowards a Conclave.

Kingsley Martin had another think coming if he thought he had any chance with her. He might be too cute for words (damn those rock-star looks), but it didn't matter one iota. She was not interested, no matter how much her pulse quickened whenever he was near. She was bound to another.

"Mmm. Nice. You don't use the hotel shampoo from the airport Hilton, do you? This is the good stuff," he purred. "But is it the conditioner that makes it so soft and silky?"

"Shut up . . . just—"

"Hold on. Save your speech for the after-party. I see our guy. You ready?" Kingsley interrupted, his voice serious now, controlled.

"Like a shot." Mimi nodded, all business as well. She saw their witness, the reason they were a few miles outside of Lincoln, Nebraska (that was it! She remembered now) in the first place. A former frat boy, probably just shy of thirty, with a baby beer gut and the beginnings of middle-age "carb face." He was the type of guy who looked like he'd played cornerback in high school, but whose pounds of muscle had turned to fat after a few years behind a desk.

"Good, because this is not going to be easy," Kingsley warned. "Okay, the boys will bring him to that corner booth and we'll follow. Square him off and then go. No one will notice as long as we don't get up. Waitress won't even bother to come around."

It was easier and more painless to enter the mind of

another during REM sleep, but they didn't have the luxury of waiting until their suspect had drifted off to la-la land. Instead they planned to barge into his subconscious with no warning and no consideration. Better that way: there would be no place for him to hide. No time to prepare. They wanted the unadulterated truth, and this time they were going to get it.

The Venators were truth-tellers, skilled in the ability to decipher dreams and access memories. While only a bloodletting would allow them to tell true memory from false, there were other, quicker ways to discriminate fact from fiction without having to resort to the Sacred Kiss. Mimi learned that the Committee only consented to the blood trial when a most grievous charge had been levied, as in her case. Otherwise, the practice of memory hunting, *venatio*, while not infallible, was acceptable for their purposes. Mimi had been given a crash course in Venator training before joining up. It helped that she had been one in previous lifetimes. Once she had relearned the basics, it was just like riding a bike—her core memories kicked in and the whole exercise became second nature.

Mimi watched as Sam and Ted Lennox, the twin brothers who rounded out their Venator team, led their witness to a dark corner booth. They had been plying him with pitcher after pitcher of beer at the bar. Mr. Glory Days probably thought he'd just made a couple of new friends.

As soon as they sat down, Kingsley slipped into the opposite bench, Mimi right next to him. "Hey, buddy, remember us?" he asked.

"Huh?" The guy was awake, but drunk and drowsy. Mimi felt a twinge of pity. He had no idea what was about to happen.

"I'm sure you remember *her*," Kingsley said, guiding the witness to lock eyes with Mimi.

Mimi held Frat Boy with her smoulder, and for all anyone in the real world knew, the dude was just entranced with the pretty blonde, staring deep into her green eyes.

"Now," Kingsley ordered.

Without a moment to spare, the four Venators stepped into the glom, taking the witness with them. It was as easy as slipping down the rabbit hole.